SKELMERSD

D0229759

FICTION RESERVE STOCK LL60

TITLE   The Englishman's wife

Lancashire County Library

30118091339949

Louis Sanders studied English at the Sorbonne and lived for several years in Britain. *The Englishman's Wife* is his second novel. *Death in the Dordogne*, his debut novel, and the first in a series set among the British community in the Dordogne, was published in 2002. In April 2003, *Passe-temps pour les âmes ignobles* (*A Hobby for Tawdry Souls*), his latest Dordogne novel, won first prize at the Cognac Crime Literature Festival: it will be published in English in 2004. He now lives in the Dordogne with his English wife.

Praise for
Death in the Dordogne

'An affectionately teasing portrait of hapless British expats out of their depth. A must-read for anyone thinking of renting a gîte in France' Michèle Roberts

'A portrayal of rural France very different from the usual saccharine tales of expatriate derring-do' *Publishing News*

'Guaranteed to cure you from thinking of a holiday in rural France' *The Bookseller*

'Complex, well told, and quietly menacing, with a barbed, decidedly anti-picturesque slant on village life. Discerning readers will queue up for Book Two' *Kirkus Reviews*

'An enjoyable spooky tale which neatly subverts stereotypes of French provincial life' *Good Book Guide*

Also by Louis Sanders and published by Serpent's Tail

Death in the Dordogne

The Englishman's Wife

Louis Sanders

Translated by
Adriana Hunter

This book is published with the participation of the
French Ministry of Culture - Centre National du Livre

Library of Congress Catalog Card Number: 2003101113

A complete catalogue record for this book can
be obtained from the British Library on request

First published in 2003 by Serpent's Tail,
4 Blackstock Mews, London N4 2BT
website: www.serpentstail.com

Typeset by Volume!
Printed by Mackays of Chatham, plc

10 9 8 7 6 5 4 3 2 1

They had been told to lock the door, but they wouldn't listen; they were trusting. When people came to see them, they knocked almost inaudibly, out of habit; then they went in and found the shadow of their intimacy hovering over the mess inside: two dirty mugs (so much bigger than the little coffee cups the locals used) on the bleached wood kitchen table, a used tea-bag in an ashtray, sometimes a couple of plates still with spirals of tomato sauce sketched on to them; if you went into the sitting-room there would be a basket with needles and reels of cotton and a few pins, all spread out beside an armchair, an open book, a bunch of wild flowers wilting in a vase, a man's jacket on the back of a chair. Then you smelt the sort of warmth that emanated from these strange pieces of furniture: the wooden chairs with arm-rests and complicated backs with interlacing curves, almost like ancient musical instruments; the deep armchairs covered in linen, striped or with more restful floral designs; the pine tables and cupboards with their half-full ashtrays and empty glasses that still smelled of alcohol. The kind of mess that belonged to the living.

On the ground, behind that door that was never locked, there were three bodies, lying face down, bathed in blood and still warm, cocooned in a silence that belonged to them alone. Perhaps they were not completely dead yet. A fourth person stood looking at them, hands on temples, mouth gaping at the sight of this other kind of mess from which emanated another kind of warmth.

The curiosity that John and Georgia kindled when they first arrived in the hamlet inspired a frenetic sort of generosity in their neighbours; old Madame Pauillac in particular, a fat and jovial woman, had come over to give them eggs, marrows and pumpkins (not that they had any idea what to do with them), and she explained that she had plenty more if they wanted them, and that it would be her pleasure to sell some to them, and the same went for the chickens and rabbits which she offered to kill for them herself, and the unpasteurised goat's milk which was an unthinkable drink to this English couple. As they had been fore-warned, they nodded politely in accurate but rather hesitant French. What old Mother Pauillac really wanted was to evaluate the transformations they had made to old Camille's house, which had been sold to them, after his death, by his eldest son, the one who had left his land, moved to Angoulême and married a girl from the Charente. John and Georgia had not grasped, when this story was told to them, that they had just heard their first Périgordian understatement and that they were being alerted to the fact that the character who had committed these three "crimes" was not to be trusted. His brother lived in a neigh-bouring hamlet and had married a widow in her sixties, like himself; she had a son of about thirty and together they "did goats" as she called it.

While John busied himself in the kitchen making coffee (a translucent suspension of Nescafé with lots of semi-skimmed milk) for Mother Pauillac, Georgia submitted to the ritual of the guided tour, even showing her their marital bedroom on the first floor. The neighbour was far from disappointed by the extent of the changes they had made to the Ferme Desjean, which Georgia had renamed their "cottage" when she spoke about it to other English people. And indeed, that day, in the space of a few minutes, old Madame Pauillac was transported to the South of England as it would appear in the dreams of two Londoners, two readers of *Country Life* and of the Laura Ashley catalogue, even though they would have hidden these publications when they invited friends to spend an evening in their flat in Islington.

Old Madame Pauillac already knew the garden, which she considered to have been neglected since this nice young couple had moved in, and she had no particular wish to see it. Georgia insisted on taking her out and asking her what had been grown there "before". When she asked her advice as to where she should put her vegetable patch, old Madame Pauillac said "there", pointing at the middle of the lawn with her brown-stained finger, "that's where the soil is best. Camille, the previous owner, you know, the one who died, he always grew his vegetables there." In the exact spot where they had set out their teak garden furniture, facing the rose bushes and not far from the buddleias, so well known for attracting butterflies.

Georgia was just as surprised now as she had been when she first saw French *paysans*' gardens where the flowers are grown in lines like vegetables: a row of tulips, then one of gladioli and, perfectly parallel, a row of irises and so on. And she had seen more or less the same thing in cemeteries (and there she had even been a little shocked by it): pathways of gravel and flowers in pots; sometimes the tombs were even topped with a sort of greenhouse complete with a metal frame, piously filled with geraniums and chrysanthemums.

Old Madame Pauillac eased her slippered feet into a pair of rubber clogs and set off again, swaying from left to right and incanting a multitude of goodbyes and thank yous, as if she were talking to herself. Georgia watched her walking away with a slight smile of amusement mingled with the friendliness this "big woman" inspired in her, and everything seemed quite charming to her.

She turned her head to the sound of an engine; it was a tractor coming towards her, stirring up the dust along the track, an ancient machine whose driver seemed to be completely immune to its lurching, sitting perfectly motionless, leaning forwards slightly, with one hand on the steering wheel. He was getting on in years, with a gaunt face and broad hands, and he wore the inevitable chequered cap with a button on the crown and a faded blue jacket which had a fine layer of grey dust on the shoulders. Georgia was standing between the gate posts that marked the entrance to the farm; the metal gate had long since gone. She furrowed her brow to protect herself from the sunlight. It was hot. As the tractor drew nearer she smiled at the driver and put her hand over her brow as a visor. Then her smile froze; the man went past in front of her without waving, without saying a word, without even raising two fingers to his cap as they sometimes did, but he turned his head, slowly, so that he could carry on looking at her with his little black eyes which were surrounded by wrinkles and completely motionless, and yet somehow loaded with an expression that made her feel uncomfortable. She pushed back a strand of her blond hair that had escaped from her chignon, and it was then that she noticed her dog beside her; he was an English setter and he in turn watched the *paysan*, with an air of defiance. She bent to catch hold of his collar to stop him running after the tractor, while with the other hand she did up the top button of her dress which, she believed, afforded glimpses of her breasts.

When she went back into the sitting-room she found John had already gone back to reading his book in the big armchair. He stopped and looked up when he heard her footsteps on the flagstones, and she was amused to see a twinkle in his expression which reminded her of what the man on the tractor must have been thinking.

This memory came back to her a few days later, on Friday morning at the market in Brantôme. There she saw several men wearing similar caps and the same worn blue jackets over white vests from which tufts of white hair escaped under the arms or round the neck. They stood in groups talking, and she realised that they often spoke to each other in patois, even if she was not always sure because they spoke too quickly for her to understand individual words and they rolled their "r"s like the Scottish, although their build reminded her more of the Irish. She had gone to buy carrots and turnips from an ageless *paysan* who was as stocky and contorted as the vegetables he sold, which made her smile to herself. He too was wearing a blue jacket and a cap, but he had displayed only indifferent courtesy. The numerous English tourists – with their white cricket caps, their shorts which were either too baggy or too tight, and their loud voices which sometimes pronounced familiar words in ostentatious accents – reassured her and helped to dissipate the anxiety that those two black eyes had inspired as they scrutinised her so, so… she had looked for the most appropriate word to describe his expression but had given up for fear of feeling the same uneasiness again.

They had arrived at eleven o'clock, a little late in fact, just when everyone was thinking about packing up. John had set off on his own to buy six good bottles of Pécharmant for his personal consumption, and six distinctly inferior ones for guests, who made do with precious little, when it came to quality at least. He was not a skilled oenologist himself, but drinking expensive wine fitted the image he wanted to create for himself in the Dordogne, and he was still secretly hesitating between an eighteenth century-style gentleman farmer and a distinguished writer in exile in his garden, rather more 1920s in style.

He put his two cardboard boxes on the ground, on the bridge that ran over the island in front of the Abbey, because he could feel a cramp coming on in his arm, and he scoured the crowd, searching for Georgia. The awnings blocked his view, he had started sweating slightly; he heard a few words of Dutch and noticed a stall of delicious-looking fish behind him; then, having still not seen her, he decided to pick his cardboard boxes back up, wondering how he was going to manage to get hold of both bulky packages at the same time without any help. That was when he saw her: she was strolling indolently between the chemist's shop and the bell tower of the little church, dangling her African basket, looking as if she didn't know exactly where she was going; she kept looking from left to right, as if she were waiting for someone to come and talk to her. He couldn't in all decency start calling her to attract her attention; they were a good twenty metres apart, at least. He tried to wave to her. No good. She was lost in her contemplation of punnets of strawberries. He noticed that she had bought some young tomato plants, some mint and some foxgloves, which were peeping out of the basket. He felt himself flushing with the combined effect of the heat and his impatience. He bent over again, tried to slide his fingers between the cardboard box and the pavement, and then to keep hold of the twelve bottles, six in each box, between his elbows and his armpits. The second box slipped and fell on its side, and he swore loudly in English. One of the locals came over to him with hurried little steps to help; he lifted the box and wedged it under one of his arms, crying "wait" and "here" and "there you are" and "let's give you a hand". They smiled and nodded to each other like two Chinese men on New Year's Day, thought John with more than a hint of irritation. Georgia arched her back, and adjusted her chignon; these movements accentuated her silhouette still further. When he eventually caught up with her, he couldn't tell her how frustrated he had been because she had in fact just been stopped by an English friend, a woman she still didn't know well but for whom she had felt an instant liking. She was a painter and photographer, and lived in a hamlet near l'Abbaye de Boschaud, in a humble rural house with an interior which now instantly called to mind Bohemia in Camden, or even Islington, in the 1980s. There were more English painters in the Dordogne than anyone knew what to do with, and John wondered when one of them would ask his wife to pose for them. He knew their sort and he knew his wife. She had studied at an art school in London, and when he had actually asked her whether she had already posed for anyone, she had said: "Yes, but only for portraits. I kept my clothes on." He was sure she was lying.

John gave another smile, well, he might as well... When she saw him coming Helen cried "Oh, hello!" as if she were surprised to see him there, then she finished her sentence in her well-spoken voice punctuated by peels of hysterical laughter; as he quickly gathered, she was inviting them to join her for a picnic with some other English friends beside the lake at Saint-Saud, at about eight o'clock that evening.

People had been calling him Jean Desjean since his mother had remarried, but it obviously wasn't his real name. He had kept his father's name. His father, a diminutive man from Alsace, had taken refuge in the Dordogne during the war and never left, eventually marrying a girl from Saint-Pancrace and taking over his father-in-law's farm, but then he died before his time, as they say. His wife, who had inherited another farm of more than sixty hectares from an uncle, later married Desjean. Since the little man from Alsace had been thrifty and a hard worker, his widow never had to worry. She had always been called the Gascou girl, Maud. No one had ever really been able to pronounce the Alsacien's name, they didn't try that hard, mind you. As a result, Jean had become the Gascou grandson or Maud's son; you couldn't call him Jean Desjean to his face, he found the repetition of those syllables completely ridiculous and he experienced them as a slap in the face. He would fly into a silent rage, turn on his heel and leave with his shoulders hunched and his hands in his pockets.

He had already finished milking the goats a while earlier when he opened the glazed door of the kitchen, startling the dog as it slept in its filthy basket. He had also fed the sheep and the two cows in the barn, then he had lain down and done nothing for an hour between the round hay bales, piled one on top of the other and wrapped in black plastic.

His mother was wearing her nylon apron and leaning over the stove, her great fat arms stirring a greasy concoction in a cast-iron pan.

"You don't have to slam the door like that," she said without turning round as she heard the panes rattling.

Her husband was already at the table, in his place, at the end, and he was filling his Pyrex glass with a light, almost transparent wine from an unlabelled bottle which he then sealed with a plastic cork.

Jean went to wash his hands in the kitchen sink, pushing his sleeves up above his elbows to lather his tanned, muscular forearms with washing-up liquid.

"There's some soap there," said his mother, still half-inside the vast hearth in which the kitchen appliances had been installed side by side: the range and the washing machine.

Jean wiped himself with a linen cloth and went and sat down in front of his slightly chipped white soup bowl. He sat half-turned away from his stepfather in the chair opposite him to show that even in this situation he could turn his back on him. He still hadn't uttered a word. The stepfather looked at him and shook his head, and, as usual, he snapped first and broke the silence:

"So… that second crop of hay? Is it going to make itself, then? Is that what you think?"

"I think it'll be made without you, anyway."

To avoid the need to reply the stepfather downed his glass in one and refilled it.

"Don't start bickering now, I can't stand it," said Maud, the mother.

"Drink?" the stepfather asked Jean because he already knew the answer.

"No."

"Go on, drink, what are you afraid of?"

"I don't want any, I said."

The old man shrugged his shoulders and turned away.

Jean watched his mother from behind and he could see from how perfectly still she stood that she was waiting for the scene to erupt. The old boy was particularly aggressive today, he must have seen or heard something which he would refuse to talk about, but which he would go on ruminating about up at his end of the table at the same time as he ate the soup, the bread and the pâté, the cheese, and what was left of the *confit* from the day before. Only this time Jean was wrong and his stepfather couldn't keep whatever it was that was niggling him to himself any longer.

"He's sold the house."

"You got the land. And you've already got a house, anyway."

Maud hoped for a moment – although not with much conviction – that she might create a diversion by putting the tureen of soup on the table, and that they could go on to something else. In order to give this hope a bit more of a chance, she launched into a vague anecdote, ready to improvise if that was what it would take: "Hey, did you know…"

She didn't have time to go any further.

"That's my father's house," said her husband, turning towards her to call her to witness this statement, and pouring himself still more wine.

"You shouldn't drink wine with soup. It's not good for you," she said.

"Don't worry about that." And he put his glass down in a pointedly noisy way. "It's been bought by some English people," and as he said this he could see the woman's silhouette as she stood between the two stone pillars of the gateway, her pale round face, her blue eyes, her blond hair and the curve of her thighs beneath her dress as she bent to hold back her dog. He looked at his wife's son with a half-smile. The latter had just shrugged his shoulders.

"What does that matter?"

In fact, the old boy himself didn't feel any additional bitterness because they were English; it didn't matter much to him if they were English, Dutch, German or Parisian (actually, that would have been the worst). He had sold the house and that was plenty bad enough. "He" was his brother. And it was most probably all down to that Charentaise girl he had married when you got to the bottom of it. A shopkeeper's daughter who ran a sweet shop and who had a handful of farms around Ruffec or somewhere over there, who didn't need another one, here. He knew what they were like, the people from Charente; when it came to being offered a glass of wine, they were always there, but as for offering it to others, that was a different matter. And him, the brother who no longer set foot in the village any more. Who did what he could to make some money in Angoulême. Fat and grubby. And lazy with it. It could all, in fact, be summed up in one sentence, which he repeated out loud: "He's sold the house."

Amongst themselves they had named this place "the lake", and, like animals around a water hole in the jungle or on the steppe, the English, the French, the Dutch and the Germans took their turns at different times of day round the expanse of water at Saint-Saud. The evening and the night belonged to the English. If some French, German or Dutch people did sometimes stay on a little late or pass them as they left, they tended to keep a respectful distance. They scarcely even watched each other from afar. At the time, the edges of the lake had not been made presentable, there was no sand on its perimeter to imitate a beach, no showers, no flag forbidding bathing in particular places at particular times. Along the edges of the meadow that led down to the lake and along the woods were lines of cars registered either in Great Britain or the Dordogne, although often right-hand drive model. If you came through the high grass, then into the woods, that was where you would find the little gathering. While the setting sun sent out its last diffuse golden rays, which were reflected in the dark waters of the lake, they would start to light the candles on the old silver candelabras which would illuminate the picnic. The cutlery was silver too, and the plates, although not of a set, were in bone china and were laid out on tartan cloths thrown over wooden tables half-rotted away by the rain, with legs dug deep into the ground. They usually arrived between half past seven and eight o'clock. Georgia was wearing her swimming costume under her dress; John had his trunks on under his shorts.

He was carrying the African basket with their towels and the salad that Georgia had made, as Helen had requested, as her contribution to the meal. It was the first time they had been to one of these get-togethers. John knew that all the others were old hands, and he was overcome with shyness as he crossed the meadow behind Georgia, watching her walk and feeling the tall grass whipping at his hairy, overly white legs with their smattering of freckles. He wouldn't have been able to say how many people were there that evening, especially as silhouettes dripping with water kept appearing, emerging from the water and hunching over as people always do after swimming, rubbing their hands together at chest height, their elbows tucked in and their hair looking like drowned rats' tails. Georgia was greeted by Helen, who undertook the introductions to the others; they were received with welcoming and distinguished barks of greeting as if in the space of an evening a magician had transformed a pack of elegant gun dogs into a club of English picnickers. They were immediately given a glass of red wine each as they exchanged banalities and niceties with these people, who still seemed to them to be just an indistinct mass from which a face, a shoulder or an arm would detach itself from time to time for a few seconds, the time it took to answer a question. People asked whether they were planning to swim and, as they weren't sure, they were encouraged to.

John felt little inclination to undress in front of all these strangers; he asked whether the water wasn't too cold, whether it was clean, whether there were fish in the lake. They answered very patiently. Meanwhile, Georgia had let her dress drop to her feet like a slave in a Persian market, and was making her way towards the water, swaying attractively with each poised footstep. "She looks like a Negress," he thought. She tested the water with her toes and went slowly into the lake, watched by John, who didn't dare turn round to see whether the other men were also watching his wife, glancing intently over the edges of their wine glasses. The lower half of her body disappeared slowly, the water was now just under her buttocks, and she took one or two more steps with an exaggerated movement of her torso before diving in, cleaving the surface of the water with her wide shoulders like a Nordic sprite.

John had finished unbuttoning his shirt exasperatingly slowly and now he was naked to the waist. He could feel his little spare tyre hanging over his swimming trunks; it was even paler than his legs, if that was possible. He thought that, in the end, there were people of all ages and all shapes and sizes back there behind him, sitting at these tables, and, taking some comfort from this idea, he drew in his stomach before braving the water, which he found positively glacial. All he could now see of Georgia was her head, bobbing on the surface of the water like a ball, some thirty metres away. And even at that distance he could see that she was smiling at him.

They came out together a few minutes later and went to join the others. Georgia seemed impervious to the pine needles pricking the soles of her feet. He reckoned that while they had been in the water, their hosts had had time to drink at least two glasses each, and he deduced this from the volume of the conversation, which had risen noticeably. They were made to sit down at a table; they were quite a distance apart, Georgia was between Helen and Dave, perfectly at ease; he could see that she was smiling and joking, but he couldn't hear what she was saying. He was put next to a woman who, he learned later, was seventy-three and called Lois. She smoked cigarettes which she rolled herself, and she watched him, screwing up her green eyes and smiling on one side of her face as if she were going to tick him off or make some hurtful remark about him. From the tone of her voice, you could be forgiven for thinking that that was exactly what she was doing, but what she was actually saying was really rather friendly if you bothered to listen.

"Have you got a glass? Help yourself. Remind me what your name is?" she asked as if he had just committed some impertinence.

"John."

"Give John a drink," she yelled to the rest of the table, waving his glass at them.

She smacked the table with the flat of her hand when the glass arrived and said, "There you are", still with the same half-smile, as if she had just taught him how to get on in life. Then Lois introduced him to her friends. He had trouble believing it, but they were called Alice and Eunyce. They all nodded their heads and asked him simultaneously: how long he had been living in the Dordogne, whether he had settled there permanently, where he had been living in England. He answered all of these satisfactorily and then asked "And you?" because that was what was required. Because he was still feeling slightly nervous, he drank down his glass rather quickly, and Eunyce had it filled up with an efficiency that compared favourably with Lois's, even if she set about it more quietly. He noticed that, up at the other end of the table, Dave was filling Georgia's glass too. She did not meet his eye.

The sun was setting on the far bank between the tall pines, and it turned the surface of the water into a huge sheet of orange with flecks of yellow. You could make out black silhouettes, as if they had been drawn in ink, as several children ran after each other, shrieking. John had not yet had time to grasp who were the parents of these children playing between the trees like some Victorian illustration. He watched them with a hint of melancholy, thinking that, at his age, now that they were starting this "new life", they too should have a child, and another thought came to him, one that he didn't really dare to admit to himself or to formulate fully, but it seemed to him that a child would be a good way of mutilating Georgia, what with the pregnancy and the morning sickness, the breast-feeding and the lack of sleep, and she would probably put on weight; it didn't matter to him, so long as she was less attractive to other men, that would be all that mattered, and even if she kept him in a state of near-permanent arousal, he would have preferred her to lose her looks if it meant she would be his alone. She could have been one-eyed and bald, so long as she was only his.

Alice had in fact just asked him whether they had any children.

"No, but we're thinking about it," he said with a knowing smile which passed for amusing.

Helen unleashed one of her piercing laughs and the whole table turned to her and asked what was so funny. John took the opportunity to study the people sitting between Georgia and himself, people he would remember only very vaguely the following morning. It seemed to him that there were only painters and sculptors there. Not all of them lived in the Dordogne permanently, but they all had houses here, and even those who still lived in England came here every year. They talked about the shows they were preparing that summer in Brantôme, Nontron, sometimes even Sarlat and often Périgueux. No one asked him what he did, they were probably too discreet.

Alice, who was about sixty, was talking about her time in Ethiopia when she had been headmistress of a school and had had to forbid her native colleagues from selling off on the black market the books which had been given to the library by the Red Cross. She launched into telling them about an affair she had had with an English colleague during the same African stay (and despite a sprained ankle). She brought her ring-cluttered hands up to her cheeks and chuckled with quiet satisfaction. Eunyce raised her eyes to the heavens and couldn't help herself smiling as she turned to her husband, Allan, a shy and cultured giant who was the administrator for a guild in London. Alice's Ethiopian anecdote inspired in Lois a certain number of complaints she had with respect to the employees of a hotel in India which had sorely disappointed her on her last trip when she had gone there with a film director, *auteur* of several avant-garde films in the late 1960s. John was given to know that another well-known English film director, a friend of Lois and Alice's, had died of a heart attack in this very lake a few years earlier, two, to be precise. And, on the subject, Eunyce ventured a macabre joke which made them all laugh. John was on to his fourth or fifth glass, he was no longer really sure, it could even have been the sixth, and he was beginning to relax, especially as the tenor of the conversation appealed to his snobbery. He asked several questions about Alice and Lois's friendship with this well-known director and came to understand that Eunyce had also frequently rubbed shoulders with him. The three of them had joint ownership of a house that they shared for the summer until leaving in September, Eunyce and Allan to London, Alice to Cornwall and Lois to Yorkshire.

The surges of conversation, the tinkle of silver cutlery on plates, the clink of a bottle on the edge of a glass, all formed the music for the evening. The shadows projected by the candle flames redefined their faces as if they were in some ancient, slightly absurd painting in which the dining-room had become the edge of a lake surrounded by trees, in the middle of nowhere, one summer's evening.

Georgia was a little drunk too, and the intoxication added another kind of light to the scene and gave it a warmth that had nothing to do with the season. She was almost tempted to close her eyes for a second or two and congratulate herself for leaving England and choosing to come here. With the help of the wine she suddenly felt an affection for these people which was almost excessive – given that, a few hours earlier, they were still strangers. The outline of the trees, blacker still against the black sky, and the moon reflected in the water, also contributed to a feeling of naïve enthusiasm that she had rarely felt before and which encouraged her to laugh at all the jokes bandied around. From time to time she would glance over towards John. She watched him talking and drinking with the three women; he too looked happy that evening, and the feeling of relief made her drink another glass. It didn't even occur to her that they would have to go home at some time and that it would have been preferable if at least one of them had been sober. These thoughts, which were a staple of all the parties and outings in other places, didn't apply here.

They didn't have a car crash. They both woke up with terrible headaches, which they did not regret.

Georgia was already up and was thinking about the night before with a smile on her lips as, wrapped in her towelling robe, she put the towels into the washing machine. John, still in the bedroom, was having difficulty getting out of bed. He sat on the edge of the bed and then made his way over to the big mirror on the rustic wardrobe ("rustic" actually meant it was a hideous, square 1940s thing they had bought in Thiviers). He scratched his head as he pushed back a lock of red hair, which was becoming a bit long for his age, a schoolboy's lock of hair like a pigeon's wing (terribly English, he thought) which covered one of his eyebrows. He was completely naked before the mirror, and a look of disgust crept over his face as he looked at his own reflection. He rubbed his stomach and thought he looked fat and ugly. His face was puffy with the alcohol he had drunk the day before, and the day before that. And that was only wine; when they had lived in England he had been known to go to the pub and drink pints and pints of beer, a memory kept alive by his paunch. If he had been told at a time like this that Georgia was unfaithful to him, he would almost have been able to understand and would have laid the blame on his own body. He could hear noises from the kitchen, she had switched on the radio and was listening to the reassuring purring of BBC Radio 4, stringing out a little patter of English words all day long in the British households in the Dordogne; they listen to programmes about gardening, investigations into the habits of English drivers, debates on the problems of education, interviews with minor celebrities of all ages, criticisms of government policies, or a new way of rearing calves, and they still listen – as if it were a Mass – to the weather report intended for fishermen which gives the speed and direction of the winds in the Irish Sea, around

Skye, in the Faroes and even offshore from Finistère (the English are especially touched when they hear that word, "Finistère"; no one knows exactly why, but there seems to be something infinitely romantic about its exotic resonance). For a period of time that seemed interminable, a woman's voice with a slightly outdated accent enumerated the wind speeds at sea, as if she were reciting her rosary. And, in reply to this background noise, John could hear the other familiar morning sounds: Georgia putting two mugs on the table, the suction sound as she opened the fridge, her taking out a carton of milk (why aren't there milk bottles in France?), the kettle starting to whistle; he even heard the sound of the boiling water hitting the bottom of the mug. She, from the kitchen, would hear the creaking of the wooden stairs as he came down to join her, dressed in a shapeless T-shirt and boxer shorts with a puerile pattern on them. She had opened the kitchen door and was standing with one leg crossed over the other, holding the mug of tea in both hands, with the top of her robe yawning open.

"How are you this morning?"

"OK, OK," he replied as he took a box of cereal from the larder cupboard and a bowl from the dresser.

"It was a good evening last night."

"Yes."

"Did you enjoy it?"

"Very much."

She turned round quickly in her chair with a beaming smile.

"Did you really?"

"Yes, of course."

He was pouring the milk and scratching the inside of his thigh at the same time.

"Would you like to see them again?"

Before he had even had time to reply she added: "Because Helen's friend, who was sitting next to Dave, you know, next to me, with the short brown hair?"

"Yes." He didn't remember very clearly.

"She's having a dinner party tomorrow night, at her house, it's not far from here, she wanted to know if we'd go?"

"Where is it?"

"I can't remember exactly, I'll call Helen, she'll tell us how to get there. Do you want to? Would you mind?"

"No, of course not."

She got up and went over to him so that she could put both hands on his shoulders. She was standing in front of him with one leg slightly bent and she looked down at him with a smile which suggested that he would have a reward for accepting. As if to confirm this, she leant forward slightly and, letting her breasts appear for a fraction of a second, she kissed him on the nose while he still chewed on what was proving to be a rather recalcitrant mouthful of cereal.

It was then that he realised that, while she had been waiting for him downstairs, she had thought of him as a possible kill-joy perfectly capable of cutting her off from a whole clique of friends to which she wanted to belong. Encouraged by the promise of the future pleasures he could read in her behaviour, he decided to dissipate this idea altogether.

"In fact, you know, those three women I was talking to last night... Absolutely charming, all three of them..."

"Lois, Eunyce and Alice?" Georgia asked with a little laugh.

"Yes. They're doing a supper next week too, and they've asked us."

"They'll be there the day after tomorrow too."

"Well, that's great, then."

"I'm glad you enjoyed it, I thought you were having fun but I wasn't absolutely sure so... you know, Helen's friend, Dave, and Helen too..."

And in the next ten minutes, while two men on Radio 4

argued about municipal expenditure in Sheffield, she sang the praises of the English in the Dordogne.

The hamlet in which they had chosen to settle had a bigger population in the summer; in addition to the permanent residents such as the Pauillacs, there would be two English women, "cousins" from Jersey who had bought a little house (another "cottage" as Georgia was pleased to call it) a little lower down; there was a couple from Paris who had transformed the half-ruin they had bought into a Parisian loft with rustic leanings (a stoneware pot on the kitchen window sill, and their garden was the most orderly); a couple from Périgueux who owned a gîte behind John and Georgia's house and sometimes came for the weekend or let the house to holidaymakers who were never seen. They would sweep past in their cars, which were usually quite big and filled with children dressed in colours worthy of advertising posters; they would be off making unmissable trips of a less cultural than gastronomic nature. All these people met on the roads and exchanged vague nods. No one could really explain why, but they didn't meet with each other, or only if the Parisians occasionally invited the rest of the village for a drink surrounded by their abstract paintings and their contemporary sculptures because they felt they had to. They knew other people in other villages, who actually didn't necessarily have much in common with them, just as Georgia and John had now found themselves some "friends" somewhere else. The cousins from Jersey hardly ever set foot outside their garden, where they were sheltered from other people's prying eyes, perhaps they were afraid that people would realise they were not really cousins.

All the English in the Dordogne have a Madame Pauillac and all the Madame Pauillacs have ended up with their English couple. Of all the inhabitants of the village, occasional or otherwise, Madame Pauillac had a marked preference for Georgia and John, probably because they had decided to settle here and because they were young. She secretly revelled in the idea that they had taken the Desjeans' house, even if the latter were *paysans* like herself and the English knew nothing about the land. She had never much liked old Desjean; she had only spoken about her dislike to her husband and he wasn't interested. On the other hand, she didn't speak about it to her son, who would have been only too interested because he loathed the Desjeans. And Mother Pauillac didn't want to encourage her son, who was given to fits of violence.

Maud was of course a poor, unfortunate woman, tight-fisted, mind you; and her son, the Alsacien's son, was a funny sort of a boy, not much to say for himself, but kind with it. Jean Desjean, as they called him behind his back. Old Mother Pauillac would have preferred to have nothing to do with them, even if she did let them into her home sometimes, and offered them a *pineau* or a drop of something, as she was doing right now.

They had arrived at the same time as Louis, who was stripped to the waist and sweating profusely. He had just been seeing to his horses in the paddock, which belonged to the people from Périgueux and which he rented by the year. He used it for a huge Anglo-Arab stallion he had not broken because he used it only for covering mares; in fact he was just explaining that the little grey mare was in foal and that, mark my words (he raised a short, thick, hairy finger), it would be a beautiful foal. The Desjeans weren't interested in horses. Because they couldn't do otherwise, and despite their feelings, they occasionally sold cows to Louis and he would take them to the abattoir. In Nontron. Not in Thiviers. "I do my killing in Nontron," he used to say.

It was Jean who saw them first as he turned towards the kitchen window. They were coming slowly across the farmyard, looking around, pausing from time to time to look at the chickens or the rabbit hutches, like children on a trip to the zoo. Then they would look up as if even the sky, up over the barns, would provide them with some astonishing spectacle, perhaps a slightly disturbing one but one worth watching in any event. Jean knew exactly what they were thinking and, even if it annoyed him, he couldn't resent them for it. Given that they were being watched in the same way from this side of the world to which they now belonged. He would have liked things to be different, but after years of driving a tractor summer and winter, always at the same rhythm, of seeing the same people and the same trees, he too, almost in spite of himself, had acquired the melancholy patience of those around him, especially his mother and his stepfather; they didn't have the same taste for pleasure as Louis, who sat there talking away so loudly about his animals, or old Mother Pauillac, who sat listening and making crude jokes.

They stopped again in the middle of the yard as if they need-ed to regain their courage before tackling the last few metres and knocking on the door. He thought she was beautiful. The man stood very upright with his shoulders back and his chin in the air, having been told to do so all through his childhood: "Look at your shoulders! Shoulders back!", like all little English boys, in the same way as French kids are constantly told not to pick their noses or to take their elbows off the table. Jean thought, without even having to look round, that all the men sitting there had hunched shoulders and were leaning forwards over their glasses.

"What are you looking at there?" asked his stepfather.

He didn't have time to answer. At that moment they heard the three knocks on the door and barking from the old dog, who had been sleeping in the sun and had only just realised that strangers had invaded her territory.

Madame Pauillac got up and went to open the door, saying, "Come in, come in, come on in!" as soon as she recognised John and Georgia, "Come and have a drink, we've got some friends here, come on in!" They hadn't realised that there was such a gathering in the Pauillacs' kitchen; if they had they might have turned back. Out of shyness. As well as Louis and the Desjeans, there was Héloïse, Madame Pauillac's daughter, a spinster of about sixty who lived in a nearby hamlet and whose only form of company was a caged turtle dove which she took everywhere with her. The bird was standing on the table and was cooing because it had just laid an egg, while Héloïse stroked its head gently. She was next to a seventeen-year-old youth with a chubby, angelic face and two huge blue eyes with a rather vague expression. He too was playing with the turtle dove, offering his finger for the bird to peck at gently. From time to time the boy looked up at the spinster and they smiled to each other, both touched by the animal's reactions.

Georgia had crossed her arms across her chest, aware that the men's eyes were lingering on her curves, while John was wondering how best to greet all these people at once. She noticed that there was a bird on the old wax tablecloth, which was so worn that its pattern was no longer distinguishable, and she couldn't help herself being both amused and a little moved by this spectacle. When she turned to the left she stiffened because she recognised the man from the tractor and he was looking at her with those same small, motionless, attentive eyes, and then in the space of a split second his face changed and assumed a more jovial expression. A man of about thirty was sitting next to him, dark with blue eyes, a square jaw and wide shoulders, but in her confusion in front of these men and the character who had frightened her outside her own home, she didn't notice that he was handsome.

They remained the centre of attention for the duration of their visit. Chairs were found for them and they sat down side by side with their hands on their knees like a couple of schoolchildren or, taking into account their age, a couple of idiots.

It was cool in the kitchen, but all these bodies seemed to have absorbed the heat from outside; the smell of sweat mingled with the stench of food with which the walls and the furniture were impregnated. Madame Pauillac brought them some *pineau* despite their protestations. Then she noticed the red plastic box made of globe shapes which was meant for eggs. "You came for the *coucous*, you must have time to meet everyone first." They didn't know what *coucous* were but they grasped that she meant the eggs and they answered with a smile.

"Do you like cooking? What are you going to do with the eggs?" asked Louis, leaning slightly towards Georgia.

"Just an omelette," she replied. "There was nothing left at home and we didn't want to go to the supermarket and…"

"Oh no. No, no, mustn't go to the supermarket, you'll find much better here," said Mother Pauillac, thinking it wouldn't do anyone any harm if she peddled her wares a bit. "And you never know what they put in them."

"It's like with meat," said Louis. "Happens I've got some lambs I'm just about to take to the abattoir, they're nearly ready. Do you like lamb?"

"Yes," replied Georgia, wondering whether she should explain that the English ate a lot of it, or something like that, so as not to make do with a monosyllabic answer.

"I'll bring some over for you."

And to show that he meant what he said, he sat back and leant against the back of his chair. He started to rub his hands across his chest, great glowing male breasts, slightly bronzed by the sun, which he massaged with his powerful hands, and from time to time one hand would go down to his round, domed belly in the middle of which the damp hairs formed a star round his navel.

The turtle dove started to coo frenetically.

"Oh, what a racket," said old man Pauillac.

"It's because she's just laid an egg, that's why she's making all that noise," explained the spinster, turning towards John. "Look," she said taking the little oval shape between her thumb and fore-finger to bring it closer to his face. "But it's empty, obviously."

"Why?" John asked.

They all burst out laughing at his amazing naïvety.

"Because there isn't a male, of course," explained Héloïse with a sly smile for the adolescent, who looked, if it was possible, like a rather simple-minded oversexed eunuch, and who was still stroking the bird's back.

They all roared with laughter as if she had made a rude joke.

Louis made the most of the interruption to get back to the subject of the leg of lamb; he explained that you had to cut the meat along its length and, turning to Georgia, he added: "But first you have to rub the thigh well with olive oil, like this, to make it tender," and with his thick, powerful hands he started stroking an imaginary thigh as John and the spinster watched, both experiencing rather different feelings of discomfort. Then Louis got up with a loud scrape of his chair and, once he was on his feet, drained his glass.

"Better get going."

"When are we seeing you again?"

"Oh, who knows… I've got so much to do."

He turned to John and Georgia and brought his hand up to his cap.

"I'll come and bring you the leg of lamb, that's a promise."

They thanked him.

Once he was through the door, old man Desjean shook his head by way of a commentary on Louis's character.

"Now, he's a right one!" he said to translate his gesture into words.

"We'd better be going too," said Jean Desjean, giving his

stepfather a dig in the ribs.

The younger man got up and for the first time since she had come in, Georgia had a chance to look at him closely, frowning slightly, almost like a little girl. Jean smiled at her rather shyly, holding his hand out to her politely and glancing sideways at the husband. John stood up and shook Jean's hand and then his stepfather's. Old Mother Pauillac saw the two men back to the door, almost curtseying as she went. The old boy went out last and, before stepping through the doorway, he just had time to turn back to Georgia; she then saw the same expression he had worn when he watched her from his tractor, in the noise, the heat and the dust. She felt as if she were completely naked amongst all these men; she couldn't hear anything, or perhaps just a buzzing as if a fly had slipped inside her ear. A drop of sweat rolled down between her breasts.

But she never spoke to John of that first meeting and the way he had looked at her.

"So what do you think of the new girl, then?" old Desjean asked when they reached the middle of the yard. Jean had stopped to take a cigarette from his pocket and to light it, before setting off again.

"She's taken," he replied.

"That's not what I'm asking you. I'm asking what you think of her."

"You shouldn't be thinking like that at your age."

"It wouldn't do any harm if you did at yours."

"I don't speak English," replied Jean, with a little smile in which the old man saw a trace of bitterness.

"Well, maybe she'll be for Louis, then, he speaks every language."

"Stop it."

"Would it bother you if she was for Louis?"

Jean shrugged his shoulders. They were now out of the farmyard.

"You're not interested in women, or what?"

Jean didn't answer. He wasn't known to have any girlfriends. Obviously he had had affairs with women, who hadn't even always necessarily been to his liking. Once, when he was twenty and had gone to an agricultural show in Paris with some neighbours, they had got him drunk and taken him to Pigalle. Thanks to that evening he now felt a mild disgust for what men did with women and physical love. And in the evenings he was often too exhausted by his work to think about anything other than sleep.

"You're thirty and you're not married. You don't prefer men, do you?"

Jean couldn't help himself flushing slightly.

"Or your goats?"

And the old man burst out laughing, a bit like a goat in fact. Jean threw his cigarette to the ground in the middle of the path, clamped his jaw together and saw a series of images in his mind, like photographs in a family album: the old man lying in a pool of blood, the old man hanging from a rafter, the old man with a butcher's knife in his neck, the old man in a wheelchair, dribbling and pissing himself.

"Come on, stop it," he said to end the conversation. But the old man was still laughing.

3

What John and Georgia couldn't know as they left the Pauillacs' house was that there was enough rancour and hatred around that table to incite murder. They had not realised that Louis was Héloïse's brother. The brother and sister didn't talk to each other. They had met at their parents' house that day by unhappy chance. She thought her brother was a violent brute, he thought she was a lazy cow. Her parents gave her money, true, and she did precious little to deserve it. Their divergent views dated back to the days when they used to walk to school together with the other children from the village which was now inhabited only by old people.

Héloïse had never married, which irritated her brother; he didn't like the idea of having a spinster in the family (he didn't know why), and he suspected her of being receptive to "gifts" from men from Saint-Jean or Saint-Pierre, he didn't know who, but he even thought some men looked at him with irony when he came across them at the café or the market, because that's where you always come across people. Just wait till he got one of them on his own to explain a thing or two. Mind you, she had every right to do what she wanted, as people insisted on saying about all women all the time, in those same cafés and over a meal after a day's shooting, in amongst the jokes and the astonishing anecdotes.

"You know, there's only one thing I regret about our cottage," Georgia said to John in the car, as they headed towards Périgueux

to go to one of those vast supermarkets they had been warned –
with so much conviction – to avoid the day before.

"And what's that?" he asked, without taking his eyes off the
road.

"There isn't a view."

"There isn't a view?"

"Yes, there's no outlook, you can't stand at a window and
admire the countryside."

She was right. At the back, the huge barn with the rotting
roof which belonged to them marked the end of the garden.
Opposite the house there was another barn of imposing dimen-
sions; they didn't know who it belonged to but Louis sometimes
used it as a stable, or rather as a prison for his horses; he shut
them in there when they escaped from the paddock and broke
the wire which was meant to act as a barrier but didn't because
there was no longer any electric current in it and he never bothered to change the battery. They owned a second barn which
served as a garage for their old car (Georgia dreamed of having
a Volvo estate like the gentleman farmers in the Cotswolds) and
which formed an L-shape with the back of the house next door.
It was covered in grey cement and was a bit of an eyesore in the
garden but Georgia had decided to plant creepers along the wall
to hide it eventually, like on the other side of the garden where
the path ran behind the Pauillacs' cow shed. The only wall that
looked outwards was windowless.

"We could knock through a window."

"It's expensive, and I'm not sure it would really be in keeping
with the house."

"Yes, I expect you're right."

While they were having this conversation, Radio 4, on the
car radio, was talking to them about the Dalai Lama. They had
reached Petit-Jumilhac, thinking that this itinerary was a short
cut. The woods at the top of the hill stretched as far as the eye

could see in a dense mass, like motionless green waves waiting to break. Georgia looked over to the right.

"Look," she said, as they passed the château at the end of the village. "Just imagine the view they must have."

He smiled without looking, he couldn't take his eyes off the road at that precise spot. He turned quickly to the right to look at the little church which stood on a hillock.

"We can see it at home," he said.

"Do you think so?"

"Yes, I've seen it. From our field, beyond the garden."

"Really?"

She was a little disappointed because it would be impossible to drag chairs all the way over there, more than 100 metres from the house.

"At least, that way we're really private," he said as they started down the incline towards La Chapelle-Faucher. "There isn't a view but no one can see us either."

"I'm not so sure of that."

Jean took off his rubber boots, which were unbearable in this heat, and was assailed by his own foul, overpowering smell, in which he immediately felt at home. He left them in the doorway and went up to his room. The only room in the house that had no window. It was his stepfather who had decided that this cupboard should be his refuge and place of rest. He had only been thirteen at the time; he had protested, but without any authority to have his views heard. His mother, though, had said nothing, and he still sometimes resented her for this. He lay down on his bed and looked at the handful of paperback books lined up on the shelves over his head. He didn't wear a watch but the conjugation of the sun and the heat with the list of chores he had already completed and those that still needed doing told him more or less what the time was. He didn't need to be precise. He knew only that he wouldn't have time to read. He took a book at random; it was one by Balzac that he had already read twice, and he thumbed through it, scanned a couple of paragraphs and then put it down at the foot of his bed. At fourteen he had expressed a desire to become a teacher, at sixteen an engineer; it was then that – still on his stepfather's insistence – he had left school. His mother, yet again, hadn't said anything. He wondered why he was thinking about all this again now, and John's face came to mind, pale, indifferent, slightly bored, probably contemptuous; then he saw Georgia's, and in her eyes he had seen a sort of curiosity. That was something, at least. Perhaps even something more than that when she had seen him leave the room, but he didn't dare interpret too favourably that slight tilt of her head and that expression in her blue eyes when she had half-heartedly shaken his hand.

She too must have read books about French *paysans*; she must have been comparing him to what she had read, and finding him picturesque. A half-smile twisted his face and soon disintegrated into a grimace. He felt a fly settle on his elbow; he turned his head slowly, it was struggling through the dark hairs. He raised the other hand and tried to squash it with one sharp movement which produced a violent slapping sound. He only just missed it.

On the way back from the supermarket Georgia had insisted on stopping at a DIY superstore, the sort that flourish on the outskirts of all large and moderate-sized country towns, providing the means for every man who doesn't know what to do with himself on Sundays to tackle pointless tasks, away from wife and children. Four or five of these characters were indeed roaming up and down the aisles of this hangar, between the nuts and bolts, the scythes, the rakes, the hammers, the drills and all sorts of metal tools that John couldn't even identify. He stayed looking at the gumboots, the only things in this collection whose use he more or less understood; then he stopped in front of a chain wound on to a winch and let himself drift into a medieval daydream, while Georgia hesitated between two spades. She also asked the salesman how to fix the blade of the scythe on to the handle, because they were sold separately. The explanation was so simple that they laughed about it together and exchanged a few joking words. John, who was thinking about Vikings and Canadian lumberjacks as he admired a collection of sinister-looking axes, heard them in the next aisle. He recognised Georgia's hesitant French. A flush of heat rose up to his face; he went round the end of the aisle and saw the salesman, a young man of average height in a T-shirt, jeans and trainers. He was shorter than John, which afforded him a secret and rather facile form of satisfaction, which he tried to hold on to as he walked over to them with a hypocritical smile. As he reached the young man he noticed that he had very white teeth and a slightly Latin look; he might even have had the look of the sort of actors that Georgia liked.

"Ah, will your husband be putting the scythe together?" the salesman asked, perhaps to confirm that he recognised that Georgia was the exclusive property of this husband.

"No, I will," Georgia replied, still laughing, as if she wanted to signal to this little male that her husband was the personification of incompetence in everything to do with physical and manual work. And he did indeed find this very amusing. Or perhaps, with this remark, she even wanted to indicate that she didn't need her husband in any way and that she was an independent woman, thereby introducing an element of doubt as to whether they were even married, which would have given the salesman an opportunity to flirt with her for longer, and in front of him to boot.

"So, will you remember how to?"

"Yes, no problem."

"OK, well, I'll leave you then. I've got a customer waiting for me at the till."

When they eventually reached the till, having picked up two bags of compost, they found another, older salesman. John felt a little relieved, but at the same time wondered why the other one had disappeared, given that he had said a few minutes earlier that he was on the till. It didn't matter. The new till operator was fat, ugly and old, which didn't stop him from ogling Georgia's breasts while she pretended not to notice. He wondered, not for the first time, how she would have behaved if he hadn't been there. Would she have tried to excite the ageing monster for her personal gratification?

On the way home he asked her to take the wheel, he too was on edge.

"Don't you think he looked like that actor?"

Without taking her eyes off the road, Georgia was thinking through the layout of her garden – for which she had Pharaonic plans.

"Who?"

"The salesman."

"Which salesman?"

"There weren't exactly hundreds of them. The one you were joking with."

Her head was still too full of petunias, irises and digitalis (they were, apparently, not easy to grow in this part of the world, which slightly annoyed her) to have sensed the danger straight away.

"Oh?"

"Don't you think he looked like that actor?"

"Which actor?"

"The one you like. In that Australian TV series. You know, Kevin… Kevin… Kevin…"

He deliberately emphasised the fact that the actor was called Kevin because, cashing in on the fact that he thought it was a common name, he was on the one hand taking a small measure of revenge on the man himself, and on the other implying to Georgia that her tastes were as common as the name.

"I don't know who you mean."

"Yes, you do."

She was pretending, for sure. He took as proof the fact that she had just switched the radio on in the hopes of ending the conversation, and had started listening to a Radio 4 programme about the great bibliophiles of the twentieth century, she who wasn't capable of reading a book without destroying it! They didn't talk for a while, until they reached Cornille, where an advertising poster for bras reminded him that she fantasised about a few particular dark-haired actors, and he imagined her being unfaithful to him with a twenty-year-old Marlon Brando, when – in fact – she wouldn't even have been born. He lowered the visor attached to the ceiling of the car to shield his eyes from the sun and caught sight of his own face in the little rectangular mirror. He immediately lifted the visor back up again in disgust, so as not to be confronted with his own double chin.

After the bibliophiles, just as they were approaching Agonac, they were treated to *The Archers*. Could any foreigner possibly grasp the fact that the British – thousands of them – listen to a radio series about a family of farmers in the Midlands who, since the end of the Second World War, have been exchanging banalities about the agricultural problems of the day in amongst a few more emotional dramas that have kept the suspense going for more than forty years? John had even surprised himself once or twice, worrying about these good people. Georgia liked the programme and was perfectly capable of following it from beginning to end after missing fifteen episodes.

"What's the time?"

"About seven. Why?"

"We're going to be late getting to Helen's friend for supper."

"Is it far?"

"Not very, but I don't know the route; she's given me instructions, but I'm still worried we won't be there on time. And we haven't taken Gulliver out all day."

"We can leave him in the garden."

"The gate won't stop him getting out."

"We'll give him a long walk tomorrow. We could even go straight on from here."

"I want to stop at home first."

"What for?"

"To take the shopping in and to freshen up, I'd like to change."

What was the point of changing, he thought. What effect was she hoping to produce. And, anyway, from what he had seen, English dinner parties in the Dordogne were hardly fashion shows. Quite the contrary; the English here seemed to strive to maintain a style verging on a sort of rural Protestantism, by wearing dull-coloured, preferably rather worn clothes, even if those who didn't actually own any livestock did try to avoid certain choices which would have had an element of pretence: green Barbours, corduroy trousers and tweed in general. It was nevertheless still possible for them to wear one of these garments, but on no account could they wear two at once. In the summer these rules were less apparent, because the temperature forced them to wear lighter, less alien-looking clothes. But blazers, for example, were out of the question.

Georgia emerged after her shower in a T-shirt with a deep V-neck which revealed the top of her cleavage, and jeans which, although they weren't skin-tight, still managed to reveal the curve of her buttocks. John preferred not to say anything and drank a glass of wine almost in one go.

"But we'll have a drink when we get there."

"Just one, while I'm waiting for you."

"Well, I'm ready."

Louis went into the barn through the door at the back. From there he could see the Parisians' garden and the closed shutters of their house. He switched on his torch; the light switch was at the other end of the barn. When the stallion heard him come in, he started whinnying and the sound carried to John and Georgia's house, where they were getting ready for their evening out. John had just shut the dog in the kitchen, convinced that he was going to piss while they were out, to punish them. He had pushed him off with great difficulty and a lot of laughing because he felt an almost surprising affection for the creature. He felt guilty for leaving him there, scratching at the door and whining loudly.

"I've forgotten my earrings."

"You don't need them. We're going to be late."

"I won't be a minute."

And she ran up the wooden staircase as he watched the sway of her hips. She started rifling frenetically through the assortment of worthless trinkets in a little perfumed box. She brought a pair of long earrings up to her ears, turned from left to right, in front of the wardrobe mirror, then decided she needed a different pair. She found one of the earrings she had in mind, but the other one was hiding under a string of wooden beads, or a diamante bracelet or perhaps even a plastic brooch.

"Are you nearly there?"

"Yes, nearly."

She gave up on trying to find the other one and decided that the first ones she had found would actually do.

That was when she heard the stallion whinnying from the

barn opposite. A long, vibrating sound that was both powerful and somehow imploring. She stood rooted to the spot for several seconds, then went over to the window and opened it to look out, still holding her earrings in the crook of her hand.

Louis climbed the rungs of his ladder up to the first floor. He moved up to the trap door to open it, remembered where he had put his pitchfork the last time and started forking the hay down through the trap to feed the stallion. That was when he saw Georgia framed by her bedroom window. She was looking over towards the barn but didn't see him despite the big dormer window which created a square of black on the façade. He stopped his work and very slowly leant on the end of the pitch-fork, took off his cap and wiped his brow with the back of his hand. He heard a man's voice calling feebly in the distance, and she disappeared.

Old man Desjean was sitting down at the table in the kitchen, which also acted as an entrance hall and a living-room. Through the half-open door he could see the bed with its flounced, pink nylon bedcover, but Héloïse refused to engage in any filth in there and get it dirty. He could hear her busying over something behind him, looking for a glass to give him some *pineau*. Their coupling had been brief, as it was every time he came on these visits. He had taken her up against this same table, a table on which absolutely everything happened, just by lifting her skirt up round her waist. After a few grunts and groans it was all over. They didn't speak much. The dove was cooing in its cage, crooning exasperatingly.

"That bloody bird gets on my nerves."

She didn't answer, but addressed a few sweet nothings to the bird as she poured Desjean's drink. From time to time a chestnut log would crackle and spit inside the wood-burning stove.

"Aren't you joining me?" he asked.

She was touched by this question, which she interpreted as a sign of affection. She shrugged and smiled, and went to get a glass from the cupboard.

"What's on your mind?"

"Nothing."

"Do you think people can tell? You can tell me. What are you worrying about, hey? You're frightened your wife knows you're cheating on her. It's not going to change the fact that she's cheating on you," she added, bursting out laughing.

That was close to the bone; he was in a bad mood, he could have slapped her. But he was the sort who was calmer once he had shot his bolt, as he called it. He didn't pick up on Héloïse's last remark, and helped himself to another drink. Then he admitted: "It's that boy who's pissing me off."

"Doesn't he do anything?"

"No, it's not that."

"Then what is it?"

"He just pisses me off."

She could see that his thoughts were elsewhere, but she couldn't know that he was worried that Jean had followed him there and that he would see his imposing silhouette when he opened the door of Héloïse's farm ("call that a farm, it's scarcely a shed!"), and that he would give him one of those superior looks and beat him to a pulp because he, old Desjean, had cheated on his mother. He usually didn't stay more than five minutes once he had finished with Héloïse; she didn't understand why he was staying on, she hardly dared put this lingering down to some new feeling for her. And that was why she said nothing.

Worse than beating him, the youngster could make him lose everything, because when he had married the old girl, the widow, they had obviously had to see the whole thing out with the *notaire*. She had said that it was to protect her boy. In the event of her death. An accident, whatever. He stood up, took a few casual steps towards the window, and managed to glance over his shoulder, to ensure that Héloïse didn't notice anything too unusual in his behaviour. He looked at the foliage beyond the tiny paddock. The house was in the middle of the woods. At the end of a narrow mud track. Two rooms, a barn, and a privy in a wooden shack behind the vegetable garden. There were leaks in the barn; Desjean had promised to come and repair them, he never had. Héloïse was not the sort of person with whom you had to keep your promises. An idea came to him: he could quite easily ask the youngster to come and mend the poor old girl's roof. He could even do it in front of his wife, to add a touch of irony which would not displease him. It would not be beyond her to insist that the boy did it, to be helpful, because poor Héloïse lives all on her own over there, and hasn't got anyone... And once he was up there strutting his stuff on the tiles and the joists, it would always be possible to arrange for him to have an accident. On condition, of course, that he wasn't out there now, spying on him. Perhaps even with his gun. No, he mustn't start panicking. That was unthinkable.

"Is it still raining in your barn?"

"For it to stop raining in there, you would have to mend it."

"I'll take care of it."

"That's right, yes."

"No, I mean it. Do you think I haven't got anything else to do? I'm going to ask Jean to come and sort it out for you. I'm too old to skip around on rooftops."

"And what's your wife going to say?"

"What is there for her to say about it?"

"Well, you know... and him, will he agree to do it?"

"If I ask him to."

He produced the beginnings of a smile which even Héloïse found a bit worrying. Even if she did sometimes have to rely on men's infidelities for her own brief satisfaction, she wasn't used to this sort of game, and even less to the pleasure it was obviously affording old Desjean.

John and Georgia were hoping for an interior version of the evening they had spent beside the lake. They were the last to arrive and only just avoided a scene after taking two wrong turnings, as Helen had not been especially precise with her directions. The party was being held by one Sue Brimmington-Smythe, who had recently sold a restaurant, divorced and set up home with a man fifteen years her junior, who seemed to be rather gloomy and impatient, a heavy drinker and heavy smoker who worked as a mason. Joshua could just as easily have been an ambassador had he wanted to, because he was the product of a very good family with complicated ramifications, his father having been until the end of the 1970s or even the beginning of the 1980s one of the most important publishers in London. He greeted John and Georgia rather coldly, mumbling "A drink... a drink... drink... drink... drink, I must get you a drink", and he fluttered his fingers as he turned from side to side like someone giving a deliberately exaggerated impression of being in a hurry. Sue was more welcoming, and they could hear Helen's hysterical laughter coming from the kitchen, as if to announce her arrival. John realised that, as a result of living in France, they had all got into the habit of kissing each other on both cheeks, so that in between each "How are you?" and its reply – "Very well, thank you" – a few seconds were devoted to leaning the upper half of the body forwards in order to press cheeks together. Georgia had had no trouble getting used to it; you would have thought she had been brought up in Paris. John succumbed to the ritual, taking a deep breath like a child learning to dive, and for the next five minutes he smelt and felt the various perfumes, powders and

different textures of skin against his face. He also had a few
moments' leisure to observe Joshua and then Dave, then an ageing
painter called Bill Eastbourne, and another man whose name and
profession he didn't yet know, as they kissed his wife in the same
way.

They were having a drink in a huge, square room which was
completely empty, had bare stone walls and half-rotten floorboards.
They had reached it by climbing up a stone staircase, and Sue
Brimmington-Smythe stood in the middle turning in circles and
making sweeping gestures with her arms as she described the
prodigious improvements Joshua was going to make to the place.
Bill Eastbourne was telling Georgia: "Helen's told me about you.
Apparently you studied art in London."

"Yes."

"Do you paint?"

"I haven't for a long time."

"What a shame, why not?"

She replied with an "oh" which barely escaped her finely
shaped and slightly parted lips, leaving this non reply in mid-air.

"You'll have to come and join us. It's such a shame. What do
you paint? Landscapes? Portraits?"

Then, after a brief silence, he leant forwards over her
(because he was very tall) and added with a twinkle in his eye
and a sly smile: "Nudes?" She couldn't help herself blushing and
looking into the bottom of the glass which Joshua had brought
her, a glass full of sour wine. Helen, who was listening, shrieked
with laughter and said: "Oh, come on, Bill!" A few feet away,
John, who was trying to explain exactly where he lived to someone he wasn't the least interested in while still listening to what
people were saying to his wife, heaved a sigh of exasperation.
Then he went back to his geographical details: "Let's say it's
between Saint-Jean-de-Côle and Brantôme, and if you take the
road to…" while he noticed Alice, Eunyce and Lois chatting to

each other a little way away, holding their glasses of white wine in their heavily be-ringed hands. They hadn't yet spotted him, and he was going to have to get rid of this man as politely as possible to go over and say hello to them. He could no longer hear what Georgia was saying. He wanted to join the group she was in, to keep an eye on what was going on, so to speak. But it was impossible. He tried to find something to say to the man he was talking to; he didn't really have time to think about it and said: "And you, do you live near here?"

The other man had already told him that he was an old friend of Sue's, that he lived in London and was only there for a couple of days because he was on his way to the Pyrenees, where etc., etc.

"Oh, yes, I'm so sorry," said John with an embarrassed smile. "It must be the alcohol."

The only reply he got was a rather cold stare. Then after a few moments, the pain in the neck said: "Excuse me, I think I'm going to try and find Sue or Josh to have my glass filled up."

The man turned on his heel and moved away. John realised that his glass was empty too, but there was no question of following him to the kitchen, even if he was likely to need a boost to listen to the conversation between Helen, Georgia and the painter, who was showing no signs of moving away. And at that precise moment Lois spotted him and waved to him. He had no other choice but to move over to that group even though, for a split second, he was tempted to reply with a nod of the head or a wave of his hand. All the same, he did glance over his shoulder towards his wife and this painter he had not yet spoken to but already found excessively disagreeable. He must have been about sixty, with his long, yellowy white hair, a deeply lined brow, a hooked nose and cheeks that looked like a Jackson Pollock painting – all blue and red.

After the commotion caused by the arrival of some more

people, who had decided to invite themselves, a second accident delayed them from sitting down to eat. As he passed behind Georgia, Dave had inadvertently knocked her just as she was bringing her glass up to her lips, and she had spilled red wine on to her low-cut white T-shirt. The wine had run down on to her chest and left a big mark on her left breast. Helen let out a piercing scream, and everyone had jostled and knocked everyone else even more than before as each of them gave their solution for clearing up wine stains: you needed salt, warm water, cold water, tepid water. Eventually the painter decreed that you had to put white wine on to red wine, and he took his cotton handkerchief from his pocket, dipped it in Helen's glass and started dabbing Georgia's breast with it, feeling the resistance of her firm young flesh under the fabric. She tried rather feebly to protest. The liquid was making the fabric transparent and her skin began to appear. Under the effects of the rubbing her nipple had hardened and its upstanding outline was clearly visible under her T-shirt. It had been hot all day and she wasn't wearing a bra.

"It's OK, it's OK, it'll be fine," she said, giggling, perhaps because she was embarrassed.

"No, wait, wait," said the painter, and he slipped his hand into the neckline of the T-shirt to raise the fabric slightly. As he carried on rubbing with the hanky you could tell that he was looking down her front.

"Bill! Bill! Bill!" cried Helen, bursting out laughing, and everyone started to make jokes about his excessive gallantry and his sudden enthusiasm for laundering.

John could no longer hear what Lois or Eunyce or Alice was saying to him. He could only feel the familiar, unbearable heat sweeping over his face; noises and voices came to him as distant echoes, even the room seemed to expand to absurd proportions. As if in a bad dream, he could no longer see more than hazy outlines of the characters forming a group round his wife, but the man who was mauling her before everybody's eyes appeared enormous. John felt nauseous and his paralysis was giving way to a rage that he had somehow to control. It was almost a desire to kill. No, the desire was certainly there, it was just the opportunity that was not. All those people around. Even in the midst of this torment he knew that his attitude and his response were ridiculous or would at least be judged to be by others. He should try not even to look tense, but that was completely impossible. The scene was fixed in his mind like some engraving in poor taste, complete with a saucy title, one of those illustrations you found in risqué books from the turn of the twentieth century: "The painter and his model", "the wine stain", "A lover of cleanliness". He couldn't turn away and look elsewhere either. Lois had stopped talking to him and was frowning at him anxiously as if he had been taken ill or was about to faint. He suddenly realised this and, barely turning to look at her (so as not to miss the spectacle provided by his wife as she allowed herself to be molested), he made an immense effort to grimace at her in a way which he hoped would pass for a smile.

It was Sue Brimmington-Smythe who broke the spell. She went over and offered Georgia a blouse to change into. Georgia refused. John had prayed to the heavens that she would accept and get rid of this wet top which now revealed half of her bosom. The painter's hand must have been very tense as he held the cloth because the neckline had been stretched so that it now gaped, and the wet fabric beneath stuck to her skin. John could still not make out a single word in this hubbub of voices, he only noticed that, thanks to the effects of alcohol, they seemed to lilt and float around him. The painter had been forced to let her go and to take at least two steps back. There were no prizes for guessing that the incident would be talked about all evening, that it would be the theme of every joke, that people would fall back on it to revitalise flagging conversations, and everyone would be looking at him and, more particularly, at her… Joshua and Dave must have made the most of it to have a good ogle at her at their leisure too.

Sue didn't stick to any specific code as she distributed her guests round the massive old door which served as a kitchen table. No particular effort was made to make sure that a woman sat between two men. Alice, Eunyce and Lois sat themselves together with Allan. Sue and Helen sat down opposite Dave and Joshua. Georgia was sitting between the latter and one Marianne Deville, who was at the head of the table. John ended up next to the painter. They were at the far end of the table on faded blue, folding chairs like director's chairs.

"Perhaps Georgia wanted to be with John," Helen suggested.

"No, no, it doesn't matter at all," screeched Sue Brimmington-Smythe. "I mean, they are married, aren't they…"

"Is she your wife?" asked the painter, who had just grasped this as he turned to look at John.

"Yes."

"You have a very beautiful wife."

It was as if he had just openly admitted that he wanted to sleep with her. John thought back to his neighbour's hairy fingers stroking Georgia's breasts. This brief touching seemed to him like a deeply embedded tattoo which would have to be removed in a sea of blood. Like all of Georgia's past with various men which she had insisted on relating to him. And the succession of violent images that followed secretly and silently through John's imagination eventually appeased him or at least allowed him to project the appearance of normality.

"Did you see, she had a little accident earlier?"

"Yes, I saw," he replied, while Sue leant over his shoulder to serve him his soup.

He hated soup. And the painter asked him where he lived, how long he had been there and where he came from in England. They were still at the half-sober stage in the evening.

It would later turn out that the painter grew maudlin with drink. For now he was asking John whether he had studied art like his wife. The answer was no.

"Are you not interested in art?"

"Erm…"

"Why not?"

"Well, I am interested in it, but only as an observer."

"So you don't have any respect for artists?"

"I didn't say that."

"What is art to you?"

"Where do I start, I, er… could you pass me the bottle?"

"Joshua! Joshua!" the man suddenly cried in a fit of artistic truculence. "Joshua, my brother, pass me yonder bottle brimming with nectar worthy of Mount Olympus, that the parched palate of this man married to the divine um… may be refreshed by the pleasures of the vine."

Everyone had turned to look at them. And Joshua had done as he was asked. Bill Eastbourne had hoped that this outburst would draw the general attention back to himself. In vain. All that was left to him then was to carry on talking to John, whom he found boring. John took the opportunity to counter-attack and asked him whether he frequently exhibited his work, in London, for example. This hit home in so far as the painter was forced to admit that he hadn't been able to display his work for… for some time, shall we say. But in the long run this was a mistake because the man spent the rest of the meal weeping alternately into his glass and his plate while pondering the true meaning of art and bemoaning the insensitivity of the public, the venality of gallery directors and the utter lack of talent amongst currently successful artists.

Joshua and Dave were talking about the bars they went to and the bachelors they met there, frequently other English masons and craftsmen whom John and Georgia didn't know.

John learned that evening that, like the painter, the well-bred English mason is a species found in abundance throughout the Dordogne. At the other end of the table, Sue, Marianne Deville and Helen were swapping memories – in their strident voices – about their nannies and their convent schools. Georgia had had a nanny and could bring her own anecdotes to the conversation. John listened. They were talking about their first sticks of lipstick, bought secretly in Woolworth's (a truly audacious step on Marianne's part because, as she pointed out, her parents would have been less shocked by the illicit purchase itself than to learn that she had chosen to make it in this shop for the poor), they talked about their school uniforms and the skirts that they tried to wear as short as possible to reveal their thighs, they talked about parties organised with the pupils from boys' boarding schools. They laughed and laughed and laughed.

4

And so the summer went on, drifting from one party to the next and on to the next. As their circle of friends grew, they would drink by the side of the lake or they would go to Helen's, to Sue's, to Mark's, to Derek's, to Tom's, to William's, to Bill's or to Billy's, and they would come across the same assortment of characters, shuffled and redistributed like the jacks, kings and queens in a pack of cards.

Meanwhile Georgia had grown closer to Madame Pauillac and went over to see her at least twice a week; Madame Pauillac's visits were less frequent, on average once a fortnight; perhaps she was intimidated by John. It was more likely that she preferred her links with "the English" to remain essentially a woman's thing.

Sometimes when they went to the café in the village, which was "nestled in the crook of the hill and dominated by its ancient bell-tower", exactly like the cliché of France they had conjured for themselves before moving here, John would spot Louis or old man Desjean inside, although he had forgotten their names and had not come across them since his visit to Madame Pauillac. There would be other characters too, who looked very like them but whom he could not identify. Luckily for him, he was not to know that they sometimes talked about his wife there, and if he had known that they called her "the beautiful blonde" or the "the beautiful English girl", it would have caused him to lose sleep.

"It'll be time to go shooting soon. Are you going to get the meal ready in the cabin?"

"I sometimes wonder what it is you plan to shoot."

"He knows where he's going to stand to keep a look-out, though, I can tell you, he knows the spots where you can see the best game."

"Funny sort of goats if you ask me."

To treat the headaches they often suffered, John and Georgia took their dog for walks, almost always taking the same route through the woodland paths. In the afternoons Georgia worked in the garden, and decorated the "cottage" in the early evenings.

The days were growing shorter. After the implicit threat of the excessive heat, other darker, weightier dangers began to loom towards the end of August: the rain, the fog and the cold. They weren't there yet, it was still warm and sunny, but there was a sense of foreboding. The summer circle of friends was beginning to shrink: Lois, Alice and Eunyce and Allan had already gone back to England, having shut up the shutters of their house and entrusted the key to the neighbouring farmer who liked to see them arrive and to watch their lives for three months of the year. And as the part-time residents left, John and Georgia began to distinguish between them and those who had definitively set up home in the Dordogne and spent the whole year there: for a start they were poorer, and more hardened too, as if the harsh winter had somehow shaped them; their clothes were darker and more worn, they drank more and smoked more and their humour was often more cruel. Georgia now saw Helen more regularly; John, on the other hand, had not really found himself a close friend, like those he had had in London. He still wrote back very occasionally, but John and Georgia soon felt as if they had left England a very long time ago and would never be able to return.

"You don't regret it, do you?" John would sometimes ask Georgia.

"No, not at all. And you?"

He would pause slightly before replying: "No, neither do I."

John had found it very difficult to work during the summer;

he had written two articles shortly after they arrived and then the time sped past and, when he added it up, he came to the conclusion that he had effectively had a four-month summer holiday. They still had a lot of money left from the sale of their flat in London. But Georgia was beginning to feel that their calculations had not been completely accurate and that, even if house prices in France couldn't compare with England, the money was whittling away. She didn't really understand why. The plants she bought for the garden were not especially expensive, neither was their food, or the wine, because they almost always chose the cheapest. Still, life here was more expensive than in India or in some fishing village in a remote corner of Portugal, from what they gathered from friends of theirs who had made these choices and whose tales of an easy life had incited them to leave in their turn. Obviously, they weren't aware that their friends exaggerated about how happy they were abroad, and even sometimes went so far as to lie. John had a contact in the editorial department of a minor newspaper which meant he could bring in a bit of money with his articles on France. But it very soon became apparent that they couldn't live off them. Calling on Georgia's parents for financial help would be on a par with getting a managerial job in a major commercial venture – it was out of the question. They could, at some point, beg some money from John's parents, but they didn't find this solution very "grown-up" and his parents were, anyway, not rich enough to maintain a couple holidaying in France by the year. All these thoughts – which had been absent in May, June and July – had eventually insinuated themselves into those late summer days like unpleasant remarks into a couple's conversations.

Louis had often heard his mother say: "Now, they're good people" and he had believed her. He had noticed that she liked the newcomers and he felt a sort of gratitude towards them. His mother was still saying: "They're nice, kind people", and he also knew that they lived in the Desjean house, and that was no bad thing. It was partly because of this and partly out of curiosity that he turned up that morning carrying a plastic tub full of meat still bright red and wet with blood. He crossed the sun-drenched yard, swearing at the flies. He yelled out to announce his arrival, and John, who was just making himself a fourth cup of coffee, nearly jumped out of his skin. Georgia was in the shower.

"Is there anyone there?" asked Louis, looking straight at John. Then, without waiting for a reply, he put the tub down on the kitchen table. He hoicked his belt up over his tummy and, pointing to his load, he explained: "The lamb I promised you."

John leant over and gazed at the chops, the shoulders and the legs, which had all been butchered and piled on top of each other as if some massacre had taken place. That was when Georgia came out of the bathroom, still wearing her bathrobe and rubbing her hair with a towel.

"Here's the lady of the house! Here, this is the lamb I promised you," Louis said again.

And John turned to her and told her in English to go and get dressed.

"Would you like some coffee?" she asked.

"No, never. Bad for the heart."

"A glass of wine?"

"Now that I won't turn down."

And John went to open a bottle.

"No, no, don't open a bottle of old wine."

"It's only a '99 Bergerac," explained John who hadn't grasped that any old plonk with a cork and printed label constituted "old wine" to the locals. John didn't particularly feel like drinking Bergerac at eleven o'clock in the morning, but he was well aware that he should join him out of courtesy.

Georgia had come back down, not wearing much but

dressed all the same, and she sat down at the table with them.

"So? On holiday?" asked Louis.

"More or less. Thank you for the lamb."

"Oh, it's nothing. I'll bring you more, there are plenty of lambs. And I'll bring you local wine, not stuff with chemicals in it, real natural wine. My parents used to make it in their day."

"How are they?"

"I thought you might be able to tell me that. I don't see them very often."

"But you should," said Georgia, smiling.

"Yep, but what d'you expect, I've got so much to do. I've just been to Spain for the horse fair. Hang on, look what I brought back with me. It's going to please the man of the house, this is," he said, getting up and delving into the pocket of his leather waistcoat for a cigarette lighter, which he produced with howls of laughter.

It was a little figurine of a naked woman kneeling, and when you lit the flame her breasts lit up and it played a little tune.

"Ha, ha! pretty, isn't it? ha, ha!"

And he kept on laughing, arching his belly forwards. John smiled in a constipated sort of way and was dismayed to see that Georgia was smiling too, sincerely amused by the bellowing laughter of this man with his flat cap.

"Ha! Oh dear, it doesn't take much to please me," Louis was roaring as he made the contraption work again. Then he promised John he would bring him back one the same the next time he went to Spain.

"You've gotta laugh," Louis went on. "We're not all like the Desjeans."

"The Desjeans?"

"Well, yes. The people who owned this house of yours. They were at my parents' house when we met. The father and son. They make a right pair, those two, a right couple, they are. Always the same."

He pulled a face which gave a pretty good impression of the permanently morose expression and melancholy attitude of mistrust the two men displayed. It was refreshing to speak to someone new and to have an opportunity to tell them that he hated them, the father and son, that is, or stepson rather, whatever, they were carved out of the same wood. He could really lay it on, they would listen to him, these English people, not like the locals who already knew everything, who didn't need to be told old stories over and over again, even if at the moment he couldn't actually say everything yet. It was at least possible to let it be known who Desjean was. He summed his words up by saying: "Anyway, with those two, you really should be careful."

John and Georgia didn't really pay much attention.

Technically, you couldn't say that Desjean had killed his first wife. He hadn't strangled her, or bled her to death, or brought her down with his shotgun.

She had been the daughter of a great fat farmer who went by the name of Planchard and owned smallholdings scattered about all over the place around Saint-Saud, Saint-Pierre, Saint-Jory and Saint-Jean. She was an only child, her father had never been able to have any more children, in fact people sometimes wondered whether the mother hadn't been playing away when the girl was conceived. She was an ugly girl, but that wouldn't have been a problem with all that money washing about the place. As Louis said: "If it's money you want, there's plenty of it there." She had become infatuated with Desjean, who worked for her father as a farm manager. Desjean's parents were poor. Their young son was good-looking. He hadn't wasted much time in seducing the Planchard girl, because he was better at accounting than she was. Then her parents died in a car crash, which was rather convenient for Desjean; in fact – given what happened next – people began to talk. About Desjean and about engines. He was responsible for looking after all the vehicles and it was a technical fault in their Peugeot which caused their deaths, up against a plane tree, which was not uncommon at the time.

Desjean took care of everything: the funeral, the paperwork, he had explained to Michelle how her inheritance worked, he was the one who went to the *notaire* while she wept in her bedroom in the master's house where she had grown up. He was even very attentive. She was thirty-five, an old maid; he was just twenty-eight. After a while he left the little farmhouse he lived in and installed himself in a room in the big house. They started sleeping together again as they had before her parents died, but they still kept separate bedrooms. Six months later they were married. No one went to the reception held by his parents and, in that respect, Michelle Planchard was not treated properly. Desjean's mother had accumulated unpleasant remarks about her and it had made her son laugh. Michelle said nothing; she sat through the whole meal in what looked like a drunken stupor even though she hadn't had a drop of alcohol. She didn't drink.

Then, day by day over the course of three years (which is quite a long time, considering the circumstances), she had watched her husband turn into a monster. He had known for a long time that she was a little "fragile". She would go for days without seeing him, then he would come home drunk from one of his mistresses, and more than once he even beat her. It was a banal story. She would sit for hours in front of a mirror, dumbly looking at her face, staring at one particular mole or line on her skin, as if fascinated by herself. Then one day in a fit of hysterics she threw herself out of the window. Desjean wasn't there; he had an alibi because at the time he was in bed with a mistress whom he never saw again but who testified for him at the inquest and was handsomely rewarded. She then left and had a new house built for herself in the south of the region. And every day he marvelled at the size of his fortune. It was also due to this that his elder brother had inherited the parents' house (which he had sold) – the old dears had wanted to console him. Desjean could have shrugged it off like many of his neighbours. But he had never been able to swallow it. And he was offended that his parents have given the house to that fat idiot of a brother instead of to a real man of the land like himself, so much more like them. All the same, when he married the Alsacien's widow, he did manage to get his hands on her farm, but that didn't change anything about the earlier business.

It was all this that Louis would have liked to have explained when he said: "You really should be careful."

Jean was annoyed with himself for having stopped in front of the Englishwoman's house. He was overcome by a silent rage at his own behaviour because he was beginning to suspect that he was no better than his stepfather. It was even worse than that because he was actually the one like a dog on a trail; his stepfather only hung about the place because he was obsessed by the house. At least that was how Jean Desjean preferred to interpret things. And, anyway, no one knew about his secret yet, even if he had at last admitted it to himself: he was in love with the Englishman's wife.

He brought the car to a halt in the yard back home and as he got out, slamming the door behind him, he caught sight of Louis coming through the gate posts. That was all he needed to put the finishing touches on his bad mood. He would shower him with his nasty jokes again and bellow at him for hours. It wouldn't even be beyond him to talk to him about the Englishwoman.

"Hey!" said Louis.

"Hello, Louis."

"Can I scrounge a drink? Are your parents in?"

Louis could tell straight away that he wasn't welcome but he couldn't give a damn; it wasn't the first time and, anyway, they needed him to sell their cows and their sheep to the abattoir. Jean waited till Louis reached him and they went into the kitchen together.

"So," Louis bellowed to old man Desjean as he went in. "Are you not saying hello any more then, you arsehole?"

"What are you on about, for God's sake?"

"You were on the Saint-Jean road just now. I waved to you and you didn't even reply. Didn't you see me pass you in the cattle truck?"

Old Desjean's face went white and he felt a murderous hatred for the horse dealer. The old woman didn't turn round; she just stayed there staring into her bubbling pan on top of the stove, but Jean Desjean saw her back stiffen. He barely raised his eyebrows as he wondered what the old boy had been doing on the road to Saint-Jean.

All through September John and Georgia marvelled at the fact that they could still sit out in the garden. John was making notes for a third article, sitting under the lime tree at the teak table which had cost a fortune, and shaded by the square white canvas parasol like the ones to be found in all the design magazines and all second homes for several years now. It was only three o'clock but he had still armed himself with a bottle of white wine to find inspiration. He thought that they ought perhaps to go and have a look at a famous village like Coulonges-la-Rouges which everyone was talking about, and to write a piece for the travel pages of a magazine that he found a boring read. The first glass of wine didn't inspire him but it did refresh him considerably. The second refreshed him even more but turned out to be just as unprofitable, in professional terms, as the first. The third helped him relax at first and sent him off into a reverie which could in no way be deemed to be journalistic. He leant back into his folding chair, made of the same exotic wood as the table, and smiled at the dog as it rolled in the grass, growling playfully. He lit a cigarette and admired the shapes the smoke made in the sun's rays.

Georgia appeared round the corner of the house, and came over towards him, still with that same slow gait, in her flimsy skirt and a vest top which showed off her tanned shoulders and cleavage. She was barefoot. She had painted her toenails an almost violent red which stood out clearly against the warm green grass. He was all the more aroused by it because he thought nail varnish was vulgar; it disgusted him slightly, especially when it was red and on toenails. When she reached him, she leant to kiss him on the forehead and he put his arms round her waist.

"Are you drinking?" she asked.

He let go of her straight away.

"Do you want to join me?"

"No, it's too early. I want to work in the garden. Helen called."

"And?"

"We've been asked out this evening."

"By her?"

"No, by one of her painter friends. Bill Eastbourne, you know…"

"Yes, I know, no thank you. I've had enough."

"Enough of what?"

"Enough of these evenings where all the men come and maul you."

"What are you talking about?"

"You know exactly what I'm talking about: Bill Eastbourne. I spent a whole meal bored stiff by him, and he spent the whole of the first part of the evening pulling on your T-shirt to look down your front."

She shrugged her shoulders to no effect, and then she counter-attacked more aggressively: "You're completely mad."

It was both feeble in comparison to the argument she would like to have come up with, and a mistake because he himself, in moments of lucidity, was afraid that his jealousy was forcing him to react to things in a way which approached madness.

"No, I'm not mad, that's too easy. And I'm even going to say that you could have told him to stop, instead of giggling as you got off on it."

She looked outraged: "What?"

"You know very well what. They were all there, clustered round you, putting wine on your tits and…"

While he described the scene as it had appeared to him for Georgia's benefit, the images came back to him with a clarity that the white wine accentuated still further, and his anger fed off the desire that he had felt a few moments earlier as he had watched her feet in the grass. He clenched his fist, and struggled to find the words to carry on – with something hurtful, accurate – but he could only think of an insult: "You looked like a tart."

"How dare you speak to me like that? Do you know what you're turning into? A jealous, drunk obsessive who watches everything I do. Do you think I haven't noticed? Always looking over towards me, watching who's talking to me, what I'm talking about, with that constipated look on your face."

It was she who had found the hurtful and relatively accurate comments, without even trying. In the end John had been inspired by the wine but not at all in the way that he had been hoping. If he hadn't had those three glasses a very simple solution would have come to mind: he would have agreed to go to the old pain in the neck's party where he could have made sure that Georgia sat between, say, Helen and Dave, which would be comparatively safe, and while they waited until it was time to go he could have spent the rest of the afternoon with Georgia in the bedroom, despite the work she had been planning to do in the garden.

Obviously it was not the first jealous scene of which he was guilty, but this time everything had happened very quickly. Usually they went through a period of making observations, based on minor betrayals. But this time he had gone straight to the insults and the shouting. The most annoying thing was that she was owning up to the facts; she knew very well she let herself be mauled by the dirty old pig. Georgia had set off back to the house. And he hadn't even had time to reply to her last, partly justified, reproaches. The whole thing was because of the wine, and he poured himself a fourth glass.

As she went into the kitchen Georgia sighed despondently and threw her head back as if she needed to breathe more deeply. Then she suddenly jumped and stifled a cry, bringing her hands up to her mouth. She had just caught sight of a man in the kitchen; he had his back to her and was wearing a blue jacket. He was looking around as if he were searching for something that he had lost on the ground or one of the worktops. He seemed huge to her; he had wide, square shoulders, and great powerful hands, which he ran gently, almost delicately, along the edge of the table. He looked at the design of the plates on the pine dresser and the mugs hanging under the shelves as if they were exhibits in a museum.

He turned round and, catching sight of her, smiled at her shyly and reassuringly. Now she recognised the taciturn *paysan* she had once met in Madame Pauillac's kitchen, then she remembered that he was the son of the man she didn't like.

"I'm sorry," he said. "I came in, the door was open. I called but no one answered so… so I came in."

"I was in the garden," she answered automatically.

The fear she had felt, the fact that this man was here, and her anger in the wake of John's little scene, all meant that she couldn't think straight.

"Are you alone?"

She thought it a strange question, even if at the moment there didn't seem to be anything threatening about him. She didn't answer.

"I'm here on behalf of Madame Pauillac," he explained. "It's about the wood, she told me she'd spoken to you about it."

Hearing the name of her friendly, motherly neighbour, she started to feel calmer and to recognise sensations which helped to restore a sense of reality (the cool flagstones of the kitchen floor beneath her feet, a few noises coming from outside, the smell of coffee which still hung in the room), and she eventually came up with some innocuous words which succeeded in setting the scene in an atmosphere of almost perfect normality: "Would you like something to drink?"

"No, no thank you, I just popped in, I don't want to put you to any trouble."

Now she even had the time to notice that he was indeed tall with square shoulders, it hadn't been an illusion she could put down to her surprise. He had regular features, a strong face and "a depth in his eyes which tempered the virility of his face", she thought, probably remembering a sentence from some aga saga.

"It's no trouble, are you sure you won't have anything? There's some coffee."

"Well, if you insist."

And he sat down rather heavily. He watched her coming and going in the kitchen between the cups on the dresser, the china coffee pot and the fridge from which she took the milk. It was only then that he noticed that she was barefoot. That was why she hadn't made a sound when she came in. He also saw that she had nail varnish on her toenails.

"It was my stepfather who told me to come and see you, Monsieur Desjean."

She noticed that he called his stepfather 'monsieur' and wondered whether that was the custom amongst French country people.

"He thought you'd want to buy wood for the winter. So um… if you'd like to buy some, seeing as we supply wood, well um…"

He realised that he seemed to be saying the same thing fifteen times and he could have slapped himself.

"How much is it?"

"Didn't she tell you?"

"No."

"It's 700 francs for a *brasse*. Or 100 francs a *stère*. It depends how much you need. I can deliver it whenever you like, because we've got wood that's been drying for two years now."

He was annoyed with himself for giving the whole sales pitch like his stepfather, like an old farmhand, but at least his logs gave him a topic of conversation.

"How many logs are there in a *brasse*?" she asked in an accent that he found endearing.

"Oh, I couldn't tell you that exactly," he said, laughing. "A *brasse* is four cubic metres, logs one metre long piled one metre high for four metres, and a *stère* is one cubic metre, a metre in every direction."

She tried to convert all this into yards but soon gave up.

He looked round the room, lingering on the fireplace, as if it would supply an answer.

"Start off with a *brasse*; you know, it's cold in winter here."

John had got up from his chair in the garden and was going over to the house. Having concluded that he regretted what he had said, and decided that he would go and apologise to Georgia, it was always possible that he might be entitled to the more tender exchanges which follow outbursts. When he came round the corner of the house, he saw Jean Desjean going back to his Renault 4. He stopped and watched him without really recognising him, but he did have time to notice what Georgia had noticed a few minutes earlier. He was good-looking.

Georgia was still in the kitchen.

"Who was that?" he asked.

"The bloke who's going to sell us wood."

She had answered without looking at him and he understood from the tone of her voice that she was still furious.

"Oh, I see, and is it expensive?"

"I don't know, I didn't really understand what he was saying."

"Why didn't you call me?"

"You were in the garden."

"Um... listen, I'm really sorry. About earlier."

She didn't answer.

"Let's go to this... um" (he was going to say old git's) "friend's party."

"No."

"Why not?"

"Because you don't want to."

"But I do."

"No, I know what you think. You think I'll act like a tart and that..."

"Forgive me. That's not what I thought."

(It was what he thought, she knew that, but he would just have to deal with it, served him right.)

"Let's go to the party."

"No."

"Please, it would make me happy."

She would have to wait a little longer before he actually begged her to do something he didn't really feel like doing, and to achieve this she had to guilt trip him some more.

"I don't want to go if I'm going to be the only one enjoying myself and you're bored all evening. Let's do whatever you want to do."

"No, please, let's go, really, it really would make me happy."

"You said you didn't want to, that Bill bored you rigid."

"No. Look, I'm asking you. Let's go. Please."

At last she announced: "I'll go on my own."

"But…"

"Oh listen, let's leave it at that, I'll go on my own, I said. I'd prefer it."

He didn't have the strength to rekindle his scene after the semblance of appeasement they had reached. He stayed at home, got drunk and didn't hear her when she came home, also drunk.

"What the hell were you doing on the Saint-Jean road?"

There, it was starting, he had become a slave to this good-for-nothing. Forced to account for his every move, constantly looking over his shoulder to check that he wasn't there spying on him.

"Marcellou told me Héloïse had leaks in her barn roof; I went to have a quick look at it."

His stepson didn't say anything. He was evaluating what the old boy had said to assess which bit of it was a lie, but it never crossed his mind that the old woman was his stepfather's mistress. The stepfather was also thinking over the answer he had come up with. He shouldn't have mentioned Marcellou because the boy could always go and check; on the other hand he had done well to stick to the truth by saying he had been at Héloïse's place and, at the same time, he was setting the bait for his plan. Then, to make peace in the meantime before he killed Jean Desjean, the old boy suggested: "Shall we go for a drink?"

"And what are you going to do about Héloïse's roof?"

"It's not a big job, but it needs repairing, it's dripping on to the big beam. And it must have been doing it for years."

"Are *you* going to climb up there and do it?"

"And why shouldn't I?"

Jean addressed a mocking smile at him. The little shit. He could go right ahead and squish himself like a piece of shit, come to think of it.

"You didn't steal anything from Héloïse at least, did you? Was she there when you went to see her?"

There he was again, completely taking the mickey. You just wait and see, my boy.

"When you've quite finished... you could do with helping people out a bit, too, it wouldn't do you any harm. Have you finished doing the cows?"

"It's done. Hours ago."

"Well, so much the better. We'll go and have a drink."

"I'm going home."

"All right then, suit yourself."

Old Desjean went back to his Renault 4 on the edge of the field, stepped over the barbed wire fence and started cursing because he had caught his trousers on the wire. His eyesight was failing with the years, he complained about it enough, and he couldn't make out the expression on Jean's face, but he would have wagered good money that he was standing there with his hands on his hips laughing while he struggled and muttered his "buggering hells" and "shits" and "holy bollocks".

Winter came on them as a surprise bearing many other surprises, some of which left an unpleasant taste. First it set about turning cold and it rained frequently. Then, without ever talking about it, John started wondering what had happened the evening that Georgia went to Bill Eastbourne's house without him.

The rain gave them to realise that part of the barn needed repairing. John thought that it could wait, Georgia didn't want to take any risks. They decided to save money and wait for the spring. But as the wiring was old and worn they felt that, as a precaution, they ought to have the electrics redone.

The winter marked a pause in Georgia's gardening activities, even if she did busy herself preparing the soil, as she called it. She nevertheless very soon tired of wheeling barrow-loads of horse manure to the garden, having taken them from Louis's barn with the latter's permission, even if, at first, she had found that this activity had a touching authenticity which seemed to come straight from the very earth. Meanwhile, John found it increasingly difficult to get commissioned for articles in England, the subjects of these articles seemed to appeal to an ever shrinking readership. As an act of friendship, they ran his articles, with more than one weary sigh amongst the editorial team, but John and Georgia continued to spend more money than he earned. Especially as with the first bout of wintry weather, she had discovered the charms of interior decorating. John approved of this new passion, and they bought comfortable armchairs covered with dark fabrics. Now John could, in secret and without talking about it to Georgia, play the role of the Scottish laird leading a rugged existence and rewarding his tough days out on the moor counting his sheep with evenings by the fireside with a glass of Highland malt in his hand and his dog stretched out at his feet. Because they were now having log fires in the fireplace which, compared with the ones in London, was indeed worthy of a castle somewhere between Perth and Skye.

When they needed wood, it had been delivered by Jean. John had gone off to do some shopping that day. When Jean arrived with his tractor towing the trailer, he found Georgia there alone in the garden. She heard the lurching of the green John Deere, but didn't really pay any attention to it; they often heard all sorts of pieces of machinery coughing, spluttering and gasping as they went past. He jumped to the ground and walked round the side of the house, and when he spotted her she was bending right over next to her wheelbarrow with her legs slightly bent. All he could see of her was her bottom, hugged by her faded jeans. He stopped dead and, with his hands in his pockets, watched her for a few moments with a smile on his lips. Then he went over, making as much noise as possible, which wasn't easy with gumboots on the thick grass and soft ground. In the end he had to say "hello" but rather quietly so as not to startle her. She turned round slowly. She had a trowel in her hand and was wearing gardening gloves that were slightly too big for her. Using the back of her wrist, she pushed aside some stray hair, leaving a little muddy mark across her forehead. Then, having recognised him, she smiled.

"I came to bring you the wood."

"Oh?"

"It's in the trailer. Did you want it to go in the barn?"

"Um, yes."

She was annoyed with herself for behaving as awkwardly as him, and she herself didn't understand why. Or rather she preferred not to know, because she still found him very good-looking and there was no denying that.

"I'll give you a hand," she said.

"Oh... there's no need, really."

He secretly hoped that she would insist. He was not disappointed.

The barn door was narrow and she had to hand him the logs from the trailer so that he could stack them inside. Their hands brushed against each other twice in the process of this task. He looked up with an embarrassed smile.

He struggled for a long time to find something to say. At first he had said "thank you" three times in a row as she handed him a log, and he quickly realised that he couldn't thank her 150 times while they unloaded a whole *brasse*. When he had stacked two *stères* in the barn, he decided to ask: "Were you gardening?"

"I was making the vegetable patch."

"There must be plenty of stones in that soil."

"Lots."

And from then on she bombarded him with questions, asking him all sorts of advice about the best compost, the best variety of tomatoes to plant, the most effective means of defence against slugs. He would normally have been incapable of giving answers to some of these questions because most of them fell in a domain reserved exclusively for his mother, but he answered all the same, saying whatever came into his head but with an air of authority, and he could see that his recommendations were inspiring in her a sense of trust mixed with admiration.

She offered him a drink when they had finished. He said no; you could do that with the English. Even if he didn't really know why he was saying no.

When John came home he found a perfectly rectangular stack of wood in the barn. He wanted to know who had delivered it, but settled for asking when it had been delivered.

"This afternoon, it didn't take long."

Once again the question he really wanted to ask was on the tip of his tongue, but he asked: "Have you paid for it?"

"No, not yet."

"Oh? When will we have to pay?"

"There's no rush."

Why was she only talking in these impersonal constructions? At least it was the winter and she was decently dressed. "Decently dressed!" He had a moment of lucidity during which the formulation of his own thoughts struck him as ridiculous. And that was why he forced himself to be pleasant over the next half hour, and to forget that a man had come to deliver the wood that they would burn in their fireplace all through the winter.

At the end of October, John had run quickly through the accounts and come to a reassuring conclusion. In November, though, they began to feel that time was dragging and they had gone out and bought all sorts of things they didn't like all that much and certainly didn't need, such as a lamp on a wrought iron stand which, from a distance, reminded Georgia of something she had seen in an interiors magazine. Or sometimes they would go to one of the region's gastronomic restaurants, emerging slightly drunk after spending the whole evening saying they had made the right choice in leaving England and coming to live in the Dordogne, and listing all the reasons why they shouldn't go back to London. One evening they decided to go for a trip to Angoulême and liked the architecture in the old town. But after two hours of wandering around the streets, which were half-deserted between seven and nine o'clock in the evening, and stopping from time to time in depressing little cafés, they tacitly agreed not to repeat the experience. They didn't go to Bordeaux, which seemed too far away because, like the countryside itself, like their neighbour Madame Pauillac and like the house and the garden, they had curled up on themselves. Without realising it, in between the expeditions to the megastore on the outskirts of Périgeux to restock their fridge, they were waiting for the spring. It rained all through April and the damp took over from the cold; the ground in the woods was beginning to feel like a sponge laden with water and going green with mould; the dog was permanently wet and they had to go to great lengths to stop him lying on the new chairs which had anyway lost their lustre because of the dust and ashes that rose from the fireplace every time they built a fire.

Alice arrived at the end of the month and opened her house in preparation for first Lois's arrival and then Eunyce and Allan's. It was a sign that heralded the advent of better weather. They went and had supper with Helen and Dave, it was a very jolly evening, and they were drunk when they left, but they didn't have very bad hangovers the next day. There wasn't that cold wet feeling weighing down on them right through till half past eleven when the sky brightened at last but still managed to stay grey, a feeling which had become familiar between October and

March. John took the dog for walks early in the morning and noticed that the sun was shining despite the crisp, invigorating wind which whipped his cheeks. Then he checked their accounts: the situation was bordering on disaster. He decided that he could resort to asking for help from his parents for the work on the roof planned for June. They found that one of the structural beams was rotten, that the work would take longer than envisaged and would, naturally, be more expensive.

The neighbours had displayed considerable interest in this work, they had speculated about how much it was costing and had come to chat to the workmen in terms that were too technical and, anyway, talked too quickly for John to understand. He would sometimes stand between two locals with his hands on his hips and imitate them looking up in the air while they carried on a conversation about the problems with the roof structure as if he weren't there. Then, because the weather became very hot for a week, the barn roof was peopled with men stripped to the waist with white shoulders and red forearms, coming and going deftly on the precarious beams, calling to each other to make conversation or to ask for the tools they needed, and watching from above as Georgia worked in her garden in increasingly scanty clothes. John had asked her to get dressed in the mornings before coming down to the kitchen because more often than not the workmen were already there. She had shrugged her shoulders and explained that it would be ridiculous to forego this ritual without which she couldn't imagine getting through the rest of the day. So she continued to drink her first cup of tea naked under her bathrobe, and watching the ongoing work out of the window, feeling quite sure that there was nothing to fear. John was convinced that the workmen talked amongst themselves about what time "the English" got up in the morning and made obscene jokes about what they might get up to in bed, or rather what Georgia got up to in bed. He would stay up in the bedroom listening to the bursts of conversation, the sounds of their tools and occasionally the thrum of a van engine, without actually managing to see the workmen on the roof. When they stopped for lunch, Georgia would go and offer them coffee, which they always accepted.

The second summer didn't quite have the same feel to it as the first, even if events and occasions more or less similar to those of the year before still succeeded each other through the weeks: a few dinner parties, a few gatherings for drinks, a few lazy days in the southern sun which was sometimes too hot, and always the buying which helped to pass the time; but now when John went to the antique shops with Georgia or to buy a case of wine if they were giving a dinner party, he had a strange feeling in his stomach just as he took out his credit card or signed a cheque. He would scratch his chin, sigh, try to picture in his mind what this expenditure meant in relation to the state of their bank balance, and every day his anxiety grew, beside the lake at Saint-Saud or in a restaurant in Saint-Pardoux with Sue and Joshua.

They then realised that almost all the English people they knew in the Dordogne had money problems and that, at least financially, their choice of exile had been a mistake. There were of course other kinds of English people, retired and rich, but they didn't know them and they didn't see them. In any event it seemed that these people tended to live around Ribérac or Sarlat; in fact they were a completely different population.

Eventually, inevitably, they found that they were overdrawn, and the news came almost as a surprise, coming from England as it did in one of those immediately recognisable envelopes from the bank. The light changed that day; the weather was beautiful, the sky was a faultless blue, there wasn't even one fluffy, white cloud over his head, but John saw a cold, grey electric quality in this blinding sunlight as it flooded the letter from the bank that he was holding. He went into the kitchen to look for a cigarette but couldn't find the packet. Georgia was in the garden. He opened drawers, knowing full well he wouldn't find cigarettes in them. She must have taken them with her, perhaps she was weeding her rather unruly vegetable patch, or just lying in a reclining chair (bought from a second-hand shop a couple of months earlier for an exorbitant sum) at the bottom of the garden. Even if he wrote an article every week, they wouldn't find their way out of this problem. He walked all the way round the house, wondering whether they could sell anything, a piece of furniture or an antique, but very quickly came to the conclusion that nothing they had bought was worth anything, a load of old rubbish no one else would want, chipped knick-knacks and pine furniture brought over from England, hardly worth enough to fill the fridge up for a week.

Georgia was sitting on a folding chair, doing a pastel drawing of the barn door. She could tell immediately from John's expression that some sort of scene or crisis was about to ensue. She thought he was going to criticise her for what she was wearing or for leading on some man last time they were out to dinner; then she saw the piece of paper he was holding before she even had time to think back to the Bill Eastbourne incident.

"We need to talk, Georgia. I don't know what we're going to do. It's from the bank. We're overdrawn."

"But how?"

He shrugged his shoulders, ran his hand through his hair and raised his eyes to the heavens.

"What are we going to do?" she asked.

"That's just it, I don't know. We've got to find a solution."

She put her pastels away carefully in their box (they were a new acquisition, he would never have believed that little bits of chalk could be so expensive) and headed for the house, asking him whether he would like a cup of coffee. There were just fifteen cigarettes left in the packet and they would all go up in smoke in the course of the next hour.

"We're going to have to go and buy some more."

"Perhaps we should be smoking roll-ups."

They talked all day, all through lunch, all through walking the dog and all evening as they demolished three bottles of red wine. All sorts of solutions, each more improbable than the last, came to mind. They needed time but it was *now* that they were overdrawn. John mused that he didn't really understand the relationship between money and time, as he had not realised that by spending small amounts over a period of time, you eventually chalked up a much larger sum.

Over the next week, John often woke covered in sweat, having had one or several bad dreams. He wondered what he was doing in this house which still didn't seem familiar to him because it was so far from the world he had known all his life and in which he grew up; he was in a foreign country, surrounded by people who, when all was said and done, would be completely indifferent to their problems. In his anxiety, lying between the sheets at nine o'clock in the morning, he was not above judging his friends and neighbours somewhat unjustly. He told himself that it didn't really matter if the others didn't have any money, they knew how to live without it, but how was *he* going to cope?... with *Georgia*? Then he felt as if everyone around him was rich; every time he saw a tractor go past he gauged how much it was worth; he would count the sheep and the cows in a meadow and add up their value. He saw restoration work undertaken by people who could afford it. He took comfort from the thought that he would be granted an overdraft for at least a month, which gave him time to find a solution. A sweeping look round the countryside around him soon told him there was no solution there.

They were asked to supper by Sue Brimmington-Smythe and there they met a lawyer of about forty who had a great deal of charm and a great deal of money. The whole evening irritated John and he came home very drunk. The following morning he started worrying that Georgia would leave him for another man, one with a job; she wouldn't be the first to leave her husband or partner because he had lost his job or his fortune (his fortune!). He thought of London, of Holland Park and of Hampstead, he didn't even get as far as Kensington or Chelsea. Such a concentration of money in that capital city, in the country that was theirs and where it would be easy to find a fat salary.

Another evening, after two bottles of wine this time, John and Georgia decided that John should go to London for a few days to see various people he knew, university friends, people in journalism, and that he would land himself some work. Perhaps with a fax and his e-mail address he would find something he could do from the Dordogne, which would keep them alive while still maintaining a degree of freedom.

They had to wait till the end of the summer, when everyone was back from their holidays. John rang his bank manager and begged him in a quivering voice to grant him a larger overdraft until the middle of September. The bank manager agreed and John and Georgia went to celebrate the good news in a particularly expensive restaurant in Brantôme.

5

On the 15th of September Georgia dropped John at the station in Thiviers. He had decided not to take the TGV in Angoulême in order to save money, and because he didn't want her to have to go all that way in the car. He was also worried that she might have an accident or even a breakdown and might be forced to call on the help of a mechanic, all alone on the open road, and to follow him into some hangar that smelt of metal and engine oil, and was papered with calendars of pin-ups showing their buttocks and breasts.

Georgia went home. The house seemed huge and steeped in oppressive silence. Outside it started to rain. It was not very warm but she didn't have the heart to build a fire. In the end she decided to go to bed. It was still early. Her footsteps echoed on the wooden stairs. She undressed and just as she was lying down between the sheets that still smelled of John she heard loud voices and a tractor engine on the track that went through the little village. She thought that she should perhaps have locked the door. But she didn't have the energy to get out of bed.

Sitting in his compartment in the train, John read a detective novel in which the central character had the same name as Georgia's previous boyfriend, the one with a bachelor flat. As a result of this he had trouble concentrating on the story, and Georgia's past kept coming back to him in between the tiny typed letters before his eyes which soon didn't mean anything to him at all. He could read the same simple sentence four times without really grasping its meaning. He wondered whether Georgia regretted living with him. She had told him that that relationship had come to an end "by mutual agreement". When a woman says that, he thought, it means she was abandoned, otherwise she would say she dumped her lover. She probably felt nostalgic about those days, that chic little flat; it had probably been because she was so sad that she had let herself be seduced by a man like him. He came to a particularly violent scene in the book which finally managed to hold his attention.

When she woke, Georgia heard a muffled sound which she didn't immediately identify as a gunshot. Then there were several more detonations and there was no longer any room for doubt. People were out shooting round the house. She didn't know who was shooting or for what sort of game; she tried to picture these armed men out in the country, working through the woods and the fields. For reassurance she called the dog and finally made up her mind to get up and get dressed. The dog's scatty movements and his excited barking brought some semblance of normality and drove back the silence. She decided that, as a special exception, he could sleep in the bedroom while John was away. It was only a few hours since he had left and she already felt as if she were embarking on a new life on her own, on the ruins of what had been her previous existence, with the objects around her just morbid reminders of that existence. She switched on the radio and the kitchen was filled with English voices while she made her coffee.

They were talking about England, and – as she drank from her big china mug, a souvenir of Devon – her mood lightened. The English voice reverberating around the walls of her kitchen masked the last explosion. It was old man Desjean who had fired.

"A hen pheasant, not bad."

The bird plummeted down and smacked noisily to the ground. The retriever was already heading back with the bird in its jaw.

"Put that in the game-bag," said old Desjean, turning to his adoptive son.

Jean did as he was told, then wiped his bloodied hand on his combat trousers.

"Not on your trousers! That's disgusting!"

"Hey, look, you can see the house from here."

"Which house?"

"You know which house."

"You mean my parents' house where the English people are."

"Are you starting all that again?"

"Yes, I am."

"Have you hidden gold coins in that house or something that you want it so much?"

"I grew up in that house."

"And I grew up in my mother's house but I'd sell it tomorrow."

"Stupid bastard!"

Jean ignored the insult and changed the subject: "We'd better head the other way, you're not allowed to shoot so near to houses."

"Oh, don't worry about that," said the old man but Jean started striding away, back towards the edge of the woods.

"Wait for me," cried old Desjean. "Hey!"

He was yelling as if he were talking to his livestock. Jean thrust his hand into his pocket and felt a cartridge with his fingers. A little tube of white plastic, a bullet which he could just as easily have left at home. It was for a deer or a boar. The dog walked behind him, waiting for the old man and panting; it still had the taste of death on its tongue. Jean started turning the cartridge over in his hand, still in the depths of his jacket pocket.

"Let's go home for some soup," said the old man. "Hey, are you listening to me? What are you thinking about? The old girl must have finished cooking by now."

"Have you finished calling her the old girl, that's my mother you're talking about."

"Listen to him!"

"Stop shouting like an idiot."

"God, the way you talk to me! I'll give you a beating for it, you just watch me. You mark my words, you won't be strutting any more. Hey, what do you say to that?"

Then, as he tried noisily to embark on a conversation with this young man whom he liked decidedly less and less, he slapped him on the shoulder and shouted:

"Come on, don't let's have a row, not here, not now! Let's go and have a drink. Seeing as you've come hunting with me for once."

"Shout a bit louder, it'll bring the game over."

"He's a real bastard, this one, come on!" and he burst into a rather forced laugh. After about a hundred metres he turned and asked: "You know the English couple in that house there?"

"Yes."

"Have they ordered any wood from you this year?"

"Not yet. It's only September."

Jean wondered whether his stepfather hadn't wanted to shoot there with the intention of frightening them with the gunfire. If it were up to him, he'd sell all their houses and go, it didn't matter where.

"Perhaps you should go and see her."

"Who?"

He knew very well who.

"Well, the English girl, you arsehole. To see if she needs any wood. And I'd like to ask them if they would let out the meadow behind the house for my sheep. Or if they'll lend it to us, we'll give them a lamb."

"What do you need that meadow for now?"

"Listen to me," said the old boy, almost tiptoeing through the tall grass in the clearing. "It would be doing me a favour, and anyway they don't use the meadow. I'll go and see them myself if you don't want to."

"No, no, I'll go. I'll take care of it if you like."

"Mmm, I thought so…" thought the old man, and he couldn't help smiling; he had an idea the idiot liked hanging around at the Englishwoman's house. He nodded slowly to congratulate himself. It wasn't difficult to understand why Jean wanted to stop him from going there, as if he were hoping to protect them. Well, let him go then.

"When she orders the wood from you, you should offer them something. A leg of lamb. Even better: the pheasant that's in your game bag."

Jean agreed.

John spent a week in London, staying with Mark, an old school friend. The friend who had commissioned his articles had made his excuses, explaining that he had to go and see his family in the North, near Leeds, and that he wouldn't be able to put him up. John preferred not to check this information especially as, in exchange for this betrayal, the friend had arranged three important meetings for him that week.

The day after he arrived he rang Georgia; there was no reply. He thought that she might be in the garden. It was five o'clock in London so it would be six o'clock in France; it was a bit late to go and do the shopping, unless she was on the way back from the supermarket. And yet when he had left, scarcely two days earlier, the fridge had been very well stocked. Surely she couldn't have gone to buy more flowers or gardening tools. Perhaps she had gone to see a friend. But six o'clock was too early for supper, and, despite their love of English traditions, they hadn't gone so far as to have tea parties in the Dordogne. At least not in the circles in which they moved. He started to worry, then his friend took him off to the pub. After three pints of beer in this environment, which was perfectly familiar in every detail from the decoration to the sound of voices rumbling around him, he forgot his worries. His friend gave him the latest football results. John wasn't particularly interested but just hearing names like Arsenal, Manchester United, even Sheffield Wednesday, Premier League and Worthington Cup, made him feel at home. After a year in France it was like leafing through a picture book from his childhood or looking at photographs of a daft but happy period during his teenage years. To round off the evening they went for a curry. They talked about Georgia because Mark, who didn't like her much even though he found her attractive, had asked John how she was. John, who was not unaware of his friend's semi-hostile feeling towards Georgia (in the hopes of maintaining their friendship, he preferred not to think what feelings she might inspire in him from another point of view) skimmed briefly through their conjugal bliss and enlarged on the delights of living in France. They were on to their sixth pint of beer and it was very hot in the restaurant. The things he himself was saying conjured the image of Georgia alone in their house in the middle of the French countryside, Georgia who, a little earlier, was not answering the telephone. Georgia who had probably gone off to one of her Dordogne English parties, to Sue or to Helen; Georgia who drank too much and laughed too much at the jokes that some rich and nicely brought-up young man who was just passing through or some concupiscent painter whispered in her ear. Jokes that were probably in doubtful taste, were certainly ambiguous and were underlined by obscene leering. Perhaps even a wandering hand.

"Are you feeling all right?"

It was as if he had just been woken with a bucket of cold water. He hadn't spoken for… for how long? Thirty seconds, a minute? Three minutes? He wouldn't have been able to say. And he realised that he was sitting there completely motionless, holding his forkful of rice three centimetres above his plate, and gazing into the middle distance.

"Yes, yes, I'm fine. It's just that I'm too hot."

"You're not used to spicy food now that you're eating swanky French cuisine every day!" And he burst out laughing, but John didn't find it particularly amusing.

When John had rung, Georgia had indeed been in the garden, noticing that the days were getting shorter, and worrying about spending the long winter hours alone in the house. She was tempted to call Helen, but she was afraid of disturbing her. She couldn't help smiling when she realised she had just reacted like a spinster or a widow who doesn't want to be a burden on couples by turning up unaccompanied. And she didn't have the strength to invite them to dinner, to cook. Not to mention the expense. It would have been indecent to have gone and bought wine when John was away in London and was going to considerable efforts to find work. She thought briefly that she too would have liked to be in London, and she regretted not insisting on going with him. She contemplated going to see the Pauillacs and buying some eggs – a meagre consolation compared to what she would have treated herself to in her favourite shops on the King's Road or in Covent Garden. But, anyway, shops were... Then she wondered how she herself could make some money. She decided that she would make made-to-measure dresses and skirts, or curtains for the English people who needed them in their new houses. She went up to the attic to look for her sewing machine, which was draped in cobwebs, and a metal trunk full of lengths of fabric that she couldn't bring herself to leave in England; now she had proof that she had been right.

She switched on the radio and listened to Radio 4 although it was drowned by the noise of the machine. Occasionally an indignant voice would raise itself above the din to enunciate a sentence which she was unable to hear through to the end, having anyway, missed the beginning. In the end she decided to switch it off, thinking that this echo of England was giving her a headache. Then she heard another kind of echo, nearer to her, regular, a sort of repetition in miniature of the sound of the machine. She thought that one of the screws must have come loose, but even when she took her foot off the pedal, the noise continued so she deduced that it must be coming from somewhere else. As it was not loud, she decided not to try and find where it was coming from.

It was only the following day when she went into the cellar and saw that some walnuts had been moved that she understood. A mouse gnawing on the shells. And from then on, every evening, Georgia was reunited with this animal working away at the same rhythm as her, but which she never saw. On the fourth evening she was almost worried when she didn't hear anything, and was amused by her own feeling of relief when she did hear the regular and frenetic little ditty made by its tiny teeth working in the dark, while the dresses and the skirts piled up on the chair next to her, not that she ever stopped to ask herself what she would do with them if they didn't sell.

John had been able to arrange four meetings during his week in London. The outcome was that he would work as a scout for an English estate agent who was looking for properties "overseas", as he liked to call it. John was to be responsible for finding properties, taking photographs and coming to talk up the charms of these manors and chateaux he found to potential customers. The only problem was that he had to spend at least three days in

London every fortnight. And there was one more problem: he would be paid on commission, but he managed to obtain an advance, with which he bought a silk blouse for Georgia in Harvey Nicholls, although he wasn't sure he had the right size and he seemed to have forgotten after a week in London that you just didn't wear that sort of thing in the Dordogne.

He went back on Sunday. On the way to Thiviers, after changing trains at Limoges, he was surprised both by how dreary the countryside seemed and by the fact that he recognised many details of it, as if this green landscape had become his own, as if he belonged there, however unbelievable that idea may have been to him, and perhaps that was at the root of the sadness he felt even though he was about to be reunited with Georgia. His time in London already felt unreal, like a series of sketches that he might have dreamed; the Dordogne winter was going to reclaim him. What he did not yet know was that he would have this feeling in both directions as he travelled back and forth between London and Thiviers every fortnight, and that as soon as he saw the Thames, as soon as he reached the vast southern suburbs of London, the house in which his wife waited for him in south-west France would seem as insubstantial as an illustration in a children's book. He would go from one life to the other, both completely incompatible, and each time he would wonder why he was abandoning the one to go back to the other during the course of a day-long train journey.

When he arrived home from London he was first and foremost surprised by how calm Georgia was, sitting nonchalantly in an armchair by the fireplace. He was wound up like a mechanical toy under the effects of the few days he had spent in a large capital city. He talked quickly, drank even more quickly and felt uncomfortable in his suit, as if he were in danger of dirtying it, here in this room which smelt of wood smoke. When, after a few hours, he remembered that he too should be asking her what she had done with her week, even if only to give the appearance of interested concern, he was astonished when she unfolded a good dozen dresses and skirts before his eyes.

Inspired by this spectacle, he unfolded before her eyes the blouse he had bought for her, and she found it very difficult to disguise her disappointment. The blouse was hideous. She tried it on just to please him. It was too late. And, anyway, it was too small. He was hurt and sulked for a few minutes, until she suggested they went to celebrate all their good news in a very expensive restaurant. During the meal he asked her whether she had seen anyone while he was away, fearing that she would say she had met some men. She said, "No, no one" and changed the subject.

Over the following week John came to understand that his trip to London hadn't changed life in the Dordogne. They went to dinner with Helen and with Sue Brimmington-Smythe as usual, like the year before, and these gatherings had the same effect on him as the countryside between Limoges and Thiviers. This was a world to which he now belonged and in which he felt at home, and it even sometimes gave him that slight stifling feeling you can get with your family. They must have felt it too, because they envied him for being able to get away from time to time. He was mildly gratified to hear people joking about the excitement of life in big cities – comments which, for once, might have given Georgia cause to be jealous.

When John took the train in Thiviers for the second time, dressed in his suit and tie, Georgia did not go home to bed. She took the dog out and decided to go for a long walk through the woods.

Old man Desjean watched her as she walked away from the village and down the hill under the vaulted ceiling of leaves, yellowed by the autumn, which hid the path from view. She hadn't seen him. She walked quite briskly, sometimes calling the dog as it ran ahead of her, some English name he would never have been able to reproduce.

A few moments later he went over to the house. There had been a metal gate in his parents' day. And his mother had grown only geraniums. There had been agricultural machinery as well, tractors and reapers. They were using the old hen-house to keep their dustbins in, and the ivy was climbing up on to the roof of the second barn, the one attached to the neighbour's. He couldn't help himself smiling. Just wait a while, wait till they have to reroof that one too. They'll see what it costs. There were plenty of them who came here and couldn't stay the course, who thought it would be easy. But these people, this English couple, seemed so strange and different to him that he could scarcely imagine how they earned a living and what forms of income they might have. After all, they'd had the roof of the other barn repaired, sure enough, and it was no botched job. He didn't know whether the neglected appearance of the garden was to their choosing or a result of laziness, or ignorance, or because of poverty. The car wasn't new. And the steering wheel was on the wrong side like something out of a bad dream, which only confirmed the fact that with people like that the whole world was back to front. He passed between the stone pillars and noticed that the glazed door to the kitchen was standing open. In his mother's day there had been red and white checked curtains at those windows. In the corner of the yard where there were now flowers that he wouldn't have been able to name, they used to bleed a pig once a year, and they would collect tubs of blood as it splattered their clothes and formed rivulets in the dust. Then his mother would make black pudding in the kitchen on a big wooden board which glowed red with blood. He took a few steps to the door of the barn. He could see piles of plastic bags, and modern-looking pieces of furniture ageing more quickly than old ones would; the colours had faded and flaked off, a whole chapter of their lives which they already no longer needed and which they had brought with them from a country he would never see and which he, anyway, had no desire to know. There wasn't a single sound in the yard or in the house while Desjean saw the past and the present in this same setting like two superimposed slides. He saw his mother crossing the yard to feed the rabbits. He ended up in front of the kitchen door and, without even wondering whether the husband was there, he pushed it with a shy hesitancy which reminded him it was no longer his home. The sight that greeted him hit him like a slap in the face. There was nothing in this kitchen to remind him that he was born there and grew up in it. All the furniture was in the same blond wood. On the pine dresser there were glasses in shapes and plates in colours that he didn't even know existed. He noticed that they ate square loaves of sliced bread, and he looked at the boxes of cereals standing side by side on a shelf. There was still the remains of a milky cup of tea in the unfamiliar-shaped mug. The chairs had wooden seats and backs, a few postcards were pinned to a wooden board: churches with square towers, a ruined cathedral beside the sea, and shots of exotic countries under blue skies, some of them with captions in English. As if to reassure himself, he went into what they had called the "big room" when he was a child and there again he imagined his mother: this time she was sitting by the fireplace on a little wooden bench his father had made and she was bending right over to watch the cast iron pots warming over the glowing embers. It brought tears to his eyes; the image was so real to him that it suddenly seemed as if his mother were somehow suspended between life and death, on the very limits of a palpable world made up of long-forgotten smells and noises. He hesitated before turning round and confronting the paintings on the wall and the armchairs with their thick cushions, which would dissipate the image. But the colour of one of the paintings attracted his attention. It was a nude. The thickness of the cushions on the chairs made him think that it must be laziness which stopped them keeping the garden and the buildings in good order. Then he noticed something white on a chair, a bra abandoned there. Then the memory of his mother gave way to the Englishwoman, leaning forwards to hold back her dog, as she had been the first time he saw her, the Englishwoman who crossed the town in her slow, swaying walk when she bought her bread, the Englishwoman who set off alone into the woods to walk her dog. He thought about going upstairs to the bedrooms. But then the telephone rang.

John had been in London for two days. He had rung Georgia three times at different times of day and had always got the answering machine. Each time he could find an explanation for her absence. He was still hesitating to call late into the night, or even after eleven thirty. Without really admitting it to himself, he was afraid not to find her there even then, and to lose sleep over it, to spend all night preyed on by terrible thoughts. He would have enumerated the possible lovers, and the places in which Georgia was carrying out her presumed betrayals, and then still more unbearable images that his mind was barely able to sketch but which would keep coming back to him, different variations but always obscene, sometimes even arousing.

He decided to ring that evening at eleven o'clock, thinking that if she weren't at home then, she might have been asked out to dinner by one of her friends. Because when he was in London he thought of Sue and Helen as Georgia's friends, and therefore quite capable of forming an alliance with Georgia that would exclude him, of forming an alliance at his expense, of keeping his wife's secrets if the need should arise.

Georgia, who was at home, didn't hear the telephone ring-ing, drowned as it was by the sewing machine and Radio 4, each giving as good as they got.

"What did you do? Did you steal anything?"

All the colour drained from old Desjean's face.

"Do you really think I didn't see you?" asked Jean with a sly smile.

This time he'd caught the old boy out. He was going to be able to wind him up for a good while yet.

"What are you talking about? Are you saying I'm a thief now? I think you're going mad, I really do. You're asking for it this time."

"Hey, calm down. I saw you, didn't I?"

Old Desjean wondered what the little creep had seen. He wasn't lying when he said he didn't know what the boy was talk-ing about. He made a mental list of all the misdeeds that could be held against him, like the manky old ewes he had sold on at an exorbitant price after buying them for next to nothing, but that was trade for you. And Jean hadn't even been there when he'd settled that deal.

"So, what did you take?"

"You'll see what you're taking, in a minute, by Christ."

"But I tell you, I saw you."

He couldn't hold out any longer and, against his better judgement, he shouted: "What the hell did you see?"

"I saw you coming out of the English couple's house."

Now the stepfather's face went dark red. He hesitated for a moment and turned to one side as if he were looking for some-thing before replying, still shouting: "You poor bastard! So what? I'm making them pay for it. So what? Then what?"

"They weren't there."

"What do you know about it?"

"I saw the Englishwoman walking her dog in the woods."

"Well, I was with her husband."

"Her husband's not here."

Old Desjean couldn't believe it; he was trying to justify himself, defending himself against this little prick, as if he were at the police station. But he hadn't done anyone any harm, had he… the worst thing was that the boy would probably go and talk about it to his mother, and she would be in one of her moods about it for weeks, wondering why he went into people's houses and what it would do to their reputation. But maybe not. He might just as easily say nothing, and keep this secret brewing like a threat, like a permanent instrument of blackmail. And it was hard to tell what his intentions were just from looking at him, with his sly little smile. It wasn't the first time that old man Desjean thought he could cheerfully kill "the old girl's son". He could feel the blood beating in his temples, he could picture him moaning under a tractor, or brought down by mistake by a volley of buckshot in the back, or – with God's help – squashed against a plane tree by the side of the road; he knew one or two plane trees that would just about fit the bill. Seeing the fierce glow in his stepfather's tiny eyes, Jean thought that he wouldn't have much trouble pushing him to the limits, and that if the old boy showed signs of violence he would defend himself, he would give him a good beating, right there in the middle of the field next to the tractor.

"So, what did you take? Were you looking for their savings? People like that don't have any."

"Stop fucking about."

Jean's smile changed and took on an edge of cruelty, inspired by a feeling of jealousy which he scarcely understood himself.

"Perhaps you wanted to give the Englishwoman some flowers?"

"Prick. Have you finished? Are you going to go on at me about this for much longer? D'you think we haven't got work to get on with?"

"It's a fine way to behave, that is, going into people's houses when they're not there. Like a gypsy."

"You've asked for…"

He raised his hand and then suddenly felt something hard hitting his face. He hadn't seen the blow coming. He tripped, the sky spun over his head and then came to join the ground as he fell and twisted his shoulder. His cheek was very hot; he brought his hand up to it and the heat rapidly turned into pain which mingled indistinguishably with his anger. He could have wept with rage. And there was Jean leaning back against the tractor with his hands in his pockets and looking at him, still wearing the same smile as if it had been carved on to his face. He had trouble getting back to his feet. And to help himself he started yelling again.

"You'll see. And you'll see what your mother has to say about this, too. You mark my words."

"She won't say anything at all. Because if you go snivelling to her, I'll tell her about your little house-to-house visits."

The old boy was on his knees in the middle of the field, and Jean could see from his expression and from his complete powerlessness that for the first time in his life he was now in a position to insult the old man to his face, to call him whatever names he liked, to humiliate him. And that's exactly what he did.

"I called you three times and there was no reply. Where were you?"

"I don't know."

"What d'you mean you don't know?"

"I might have gone out shopping, or been in the garden or walking the dog."

"Because you walk the dog?"

"Of course."

"In the woods? In the middle of the shooting season? You're completely mad. You must have heard about shooting accidents, for goodness' sake."

"During the week they only shoot on Wednesdays."

"Even so… it's dangerous."

"No, it isn't."

"Anyway, they're always completely plastered when they go out shooting, even at ten o'clock in the morning."

John couldn't grasp the fact that the men out shooting and their neighbours, whom he knew and greeted every time he met them, were the same people, the same husbands and fathers, the same farm workers who chatted and joked in the bar, and had eventually accepted him as they had accepted all the English people in the region. He thought of them as an army (and they actually often wore combat trousers) working their way across the countryside, drunk on blood, death and wine, likely to rape any woman who ventured into the undergrowth and breathe their garlic-laden breath over her in the process. Because that was in fact the particular kind of shooting accident that he feared the most.

"And, anyway, the dog does need walking."

She had it in her to battle every inch of the way in a conversation, usually using simple and unassailable arguments until he had no other choice than to take refuge in sulking.

It was breakfast time on the day after John had come home. She had been to fetch him from Thiviers on the train at quarter to ten. They had talked about one thing and another, and John had deployed considerable resources to restrain himself from straight away mentioning his unanswered calls. She had said that she was tired and had gone to bed very early. He had followed her up and she had explained that she wanted to sleep, and she had turned her back on him. John hadn't been feeling tired; he went back down to the sitting-room in his boxer shorts and his over-large T-shirt, he sat down by the fire, which was gradually going out, and he drank whisky as he wondered why she was being so cold towards him on the evening he had come home after a long separation; each explanation which presented itself with the successive mouthfuls of whisky seemed unpleasant. He had thought about sleeping in the chair to indicate his disappointment – even anger – to her when she woke to find his side of the bed deserted the following morning. But, because it was too uncomfortable, he had eventually gone upstairs rather hesitantly, being careful not to wake her.

"And why do you never call me in London? At Mark's flat."

"International calls are expensive."

"Well, yes, but every now and then just so that we can talk to each other."

"I'll call you next time then, if you like."

She stood up, went over to him and kissed his ear, thereby cutting short his recriminations.

"Hey, Louis!"

"Hey, Marcellou!"

"So, how are things?"

"You find me as you see me. So, is it your round?"

"Come on then, what are you having?"

"A pastis."

"Michel, could we have a couple of Ricards, please. So, where have you been then?"

"I was over at my mother's house, tch, I took a drink off her too."

Marcellou shook his head without saying a word, as if he were thinking that – had he known – he would have made Louis pay.

He himself was still sober, it was only half past eleven and he had only had three drinks.

They started to laugh.

"Tch, d'you know what I saw?"

"What did you see?"

"Well…"

"You didn't see anything at all, it's another one of your stories."

"Well, if you don't want me to tell you…"

"More of your rubbish."

"Yes, my rubbish, that's right."

He was beginning to worry about Louis's indifference, because even if his lack of interest was not totally convincing and if the game of waiting and doubting that they were both playing was fairly clear, all it would take would be for another customer to come in now and his story would have to fall by the wayside. And even though he was prepared to divulge what he had seen to Louis, who constituted an exceptional propagator of information, he was nevertheless not ready to announce it to a whole room full of people. The *patron*, with his cloth over his shoulder, was pretending to look outside to see whether there was a car waiting at the petrol pump, because he was also the pump attendant.

On the other side of the road a group of men had gathered, three Basque berets and three blue jackets forming a triangle. The little black platforms created by their berets tilted back and forth slowly as they bemoaned some blight of nature, like the rain or the sun or the rising boar population, which was devastating the maize crop. One of these three men might cross the street at any moment and come into the café with a noisy greeting. If it should be old Thomas, Marcellou would have to give up on his story. So he turned suddenly to Louis with a frown and announced: "I saw that Jean Desjean giving the old boy a punch in the face."

"What did you say?"

"Well, tch, I was at Combeau, in the woods, I'd just got to the end of the path and in the middle of the field, there, I saw that boy giving old Desjean a good thrashing."

"Whoa!"

"Well, you wouldn't believe it, but I'm telling you."

Even the *patron* of the café hadn't managed to keep his composure, he had turned to face Marcellou and had raised his eyebrows.

"He didn't?"

"He gave him a good punch, I tell you. And the lad was laughing about it. He was making fun of him, I swear to you."

"What were they talking about?"

"I couldn't hear. I was too far away. They were down at the bottom over by Combeau."

Louis said nothing for a while as he thought about this new information. After the surprise, he experienced a degree of pleasure, indicated by a slight smile followed by a resounding "Ha!" as he clapped Marcellou on the shoulder. He was wondering what might have provoked this scene. The two men hated each other, that was clear. But for them to come to blows was quite another thing. It was more than likely that one of them had told the other something, or that the old boy had tried to force the lad to do something he didn't want to. There were lots of stories circulating about the old boy. Louis had peddled a few of them himself. They must be half-true or maybe not quite that much. The trick was to disentangle the true ones from the fabricated ones. And to find which of them had given rise to this incident. Despite his laughter, Louis felt slightly uncomfortable although he didn't let it show, because he knew that at the end of the day, this was in fact more bad news than good. On the other hand, he didn't know exactly why.

★

Sue Brimmington-Smythe knew everyone. She arrived at John and Georgia's house late in the morning, probably shortly after she had got up. She walked slowly towards the door, wrapped in a flowery shawl which had seen better days, and looking at the house as if she had come to buy it. She saw John first and gave him a radiant smile. He was feeding the dog, and the animal was whirling round him, barking and standing on its hind legs.

Georgia offered Sue something to drink straight away. The conversation took a while to get under way and Georgia eventually realised that it was because of Radio 4: they were having to shout over a programme about the decline of red squirrels in the British countryside in order to make themselves heard. When the kettle had done its whistling, they finally grasped that Sue was talking about a friend of hers who had a chateau and who had made it his speciality to spot manor houses and other nice properties which were worthy of being restored and sold, particularly to English buyers. She had thought that it would be useful for John to meet him and she had arranged for all of them to be invited to lunch at the chateau the next day.

"Tomorrow? Isn't that a bit soon?" asked John.

"Ashley's like that," Sue replied with a sweeping gesture which implied that he would not stop at any kind of extravagance.

The following day John and Georgia got up at about half past ten and then went into a bout of frenetic activity in the bathroom so as not to be late meeting Sue, because the chateau was an hour's drive away. John had just climbed out of the bath and was drying himself on the damp towel Georgia had used when he noticed that she was leaning forwards in front of the mirror. Arching her back as she always did, she was putting on lipstick.

"Are you putting make-up on?" he asked, so aggressively that she was taken aback.

"Well, yes."

"Since when have you been doing that?"

"Why on earth are you asking me that?"

"But you never wear make-up. Anyway, you know I don't like it."

"You don't like what?"

"Well, make-up. I prefer um… a more natural look."

There was a pause, she looked at him despairingly, still holding her lipstick in her bent arm, just ten centimetres from her mouth, as if she had been petrified halfway through what she was doing. She suddenly realised that he didn't even know she some-times wore make-up; he was incapable of differentiating between the days when she put on face powder and eye shadow and the others when she stuck to her "natural" colouring, as he put it.

"Why are you looking at me like that?" he asked, slightly irritated.

It would have taken too long to explain and she made do with saying: "I don't understand."

"I've just told you I don't like make-up. Why are you putting make-up on today?"

Then, resorting to sarcasm and with a particularly nasty little smile, he added: "Because we're going for lunch in a chateau? Are you impressed by that? You're laying it on a bit, aren't you?"

He was standing naked in the bathroom with his towel round his neck. His skin looked whiter than ever under the harsh light of the single bulb reflected off the tiling. He caught sight of his body in the mirror and shrugged his shoulders with a grind of his teeth. She turned back without a word and finished painting her lips, then pulled all sorts of faces to make sure the colour was spread evenly.

"You know perfectly well that I sometimes wear make-up," she said in a neutral voice, "when I feel tired. I don't know, it makes me feel I've got more energy, it's stupid, but it makes me… I don't know? Don't you like it?"

"I prefer you when you look natural."

She would have found it difficult to describe her feelings at that precise moment. The surprise had passed, or rather the effects of the surprise, and they were now reduced to a distant backdrop to her thoughts which comprised a mixture of impatience, probably some contempt and perhaps even some hate, no, rather a kind of disgust for this white, slightly flabby face, and for the words coming out of its mouth like irritating and absurd barks. To wind him up, she put on her most showy earrings and, if she had had time, she would have changed into a much more provocative outfit than the simple cotton sweater she had chosen.

She was at it again, yelling at him and making fun of him. Reminding him he was afraid of Louis, and a voice inside himself echoed Héloïse's, telling him she was right. He no longer knew which way to turn, or where to look so as not to hear it. He had turned his back on her some minutes ago already. And there was the bird cooing in its cage as if it were laughing, or as if it kept saying, "You see, you see, she's right."

"You don't feel so full of yourself, do you now, when I talk about my brother."

Now, that was new, she usually said "Louis". Now it was her brother. Fancy that.

"I'm going to need some money," she added, "you'll have to give me some."

He was still looking out of the window and still couldn't see anything but trees and grass. He didn't know what she was up to behind him, and he didn't want to know, for that matter. He didn't know what to say either, so he decided to shout as if he were dealing with a stubborn animal.

"Hey! Have you finished? You watch out."

"Oh yes, you be clever. I wonder what you'd do if my brother came to talk you through one or two things."

He wondered whether she was in cahoots with Louis to get his money out of him. He had been treated to this same scene every time he went to see her for weeks now. It was like with the boy. They were all at it, trying to bring him down. They were in on it together. And she was still the one with the best arsenal.

He half-turned to watch her. She was wiping her hands on the cloth that was tied at her waist, held there with an old nappy pin. Then she sat down at the end of the table, sitting like a man, with her legs spread on the chair. She had taken her denture out and was smiling at him as if she wanted to humiliate him – not herself but him – with her own ugliness by saying: "Look at me, have a good look, and that's your mistress." And she announced out loud: "You won't get rid of me that easily. You'll do as I say. I mean, what if old Maud or Louis found out a few things about you… and that wretched boy, Jean Desjean." Then she laughed, a really stupid laugh; he even thought she was putting it on.

With a mechanical gesture, he pushed his hat backwards and stroked the back of his neck, then he put his hand in his pocket and felt the handle of his knife.

The outside wall which sheltered the manor house from view had been sandblasted and the yellow stone now looked rather garish, almost artificial, as did the wooden gate which had been added recently; it was too heavily varnished, too shiny despite the six months of rain and drizzle that had fallen on it. Inside the walls, gravel pathways ran round isolated flower beds which looked like islands of colour in the middle of the sea of beige pebbles. "Too much money can damage your sense of taste," thought John, for once satisfied about his impoverished state. The gravel crunched under their shoes like in some French film about provincial life, and Georgia marvelled at the particularly steep pitch of the Périgordian roof, she oo-ed and ah-ed about the dovecot a little further on, and admired the pristine-looking eighteenth-century barns built around a courtyard.

There was a clown standing at the front door of the manor, wearing a purple velvet smoking jacket which was slightly worn – but not quite enough to look truly aristocratic. This was Ashley, the owner. He was short and very fat, and there was a flabbiness in his features which was more reminiscent of a Buddha than a bulldog; he had crossed his dimpled fingers over his belly and was crying: "Hello, hello, hello." He put his fat lips onto Sue's cheek, took her by the shoulders and made such an exaggerated "mwa" of a kiss that it became funny. He turned to John and Georgia with a "Ha!" which could have been interpreted in any number of different ways, then led everyone inside.

"The *bonne* was busy today," he explained, using the French word, which he felt was so much more picturesque and romantic than "maid", "so I will be doing the serving, which is no bad thing because we'll all get more. She worries about my health."

He skipped about on his little feet, fluttering around a pedestal table, taking the lids off cut-crystal decanters with almost obscene dexterity. The drawing-room was cluttered with armchairs in all shapes and sizes – tall, wing-backed ones, squat, low-slung ones, Chesterfields and Voltaires – but everyone remained standing, glass in hand, almost on guard, as they exchanged niceties, leaning forwards slightly from time to time like Prussian soldiers before an officer. The carpet was thick and dark, and through the arched windows carved of the same too-yellow stone they could see a sad little drizzle. Strangely, there were not too many hunting scenes on the walls, and the usual Victorian engravings of horses were absent as were portraits of dogs; on the other hand there were three borzois languishing on the carpet and on a meridienne reserved for them alone, like rather arrogant, scrawny prostitutes. Ashley never tired of explaining how agile and cruel these creatures were. They were so very different from their owner that the contrast could hardly fail to be comic; he would have looked more at home with an overfed toy poodle or a pug. He often stopped halfway through a sentence and turned to these creatures and addressed all sorts of sweet nothings to them, pouting his wet, red mouth. Then he laughed at himself, with the complicity of his guests. He told them that his dogs had once brought home the blood-splattered haunch of a roe deer. John turned to Georgia several times to catch her eye and try to discern what she thought of their host or his house, but she was not looking at him; she was clearly admiring the Victorian display cabinets full of pink and white porcelain ornaments, and the contours of the backrest of a chair that she followed with the tips of her fingers, as if all this luxury could incite her to some sort of lascivious abandon.

They were on to their second round of drinks; John had chosen whisky rather than wine and, as he had an empty stomach, this particular room in this particular manor house, the fact that Sue and Joshua were there, and the obese little man himself all began to seem like a dream that was both comforting and sluggish. Ashley was making jokes about his own ugliness, about his short little legs, his fat cheeks, his bulging tummy and his stumpy fingers, and everyone was laughing. John joined in with them as if detached from himself, as if he were watching himself with the others, looking down from an imaginary mezzanine. Sue explained to Ashley – as if she had not already – that John worked for a London estate agent and that he was particularly interested in manor houses and chateaux for his "extensive client list". Ashley determined that they should meet another day, but that they should not talk shop now so as not to ruin the lunch.

While Ashley served the wine he asked Georgia what she did with herself in the Périgord. She explained that she spent her time sewing and gardening, and Ashley behaved as if he had never heard anything so wonderful. He took a mouthful of wine, wiped his lips and chin, and explained that he needed some curtains. They agreed to meet again, and John was delighted to think of the imminent influx of money that his order would bring. Sue, Joshua and Ashley exchanged news about people that John and Georgia didn't know, people who lived in London and moved in a social circle above theirs. As the wine was flowing well, they were soon on to the third bottle, and Joshua was opening a fourth at Ashley's request, when Sue turned to Georgia and said: "I rang your house the other day and someone French answered. A man...oh!"

She burst out laughing and Ashley picked up on her "oh", raising his eyebrows and pulling a face.

"I asked whether you were there," Sue went on, "and he said 'no, she's gone out, I'm her cousin'." (Laugh.) "Her cousin? I wondered what on earth was going on."

Georgia looked amazed and amused; she asked Sue to repeat what had happened, shrugged her shoulders and raised her eyebrows.

"When was it?"

"I don't know, it must have been last week or a bit before. I forgot to tell you about it. But... hmmm... I was intrigued. Actually, it must have been when John was in London. John!" she exclaimed, "you should be careful!"

John was befuddled by the wine and it took him several seconds to grasp exactly what Sue had said. He was helped along the way by the succession of jokes that ensued about cousins and men's voices. Georgia was laughing too and simpering. A thousand questions clamoured in John's head, and there was one answer which offered itself immediately: it had been a mistake, Sue had dialled the wrong number, had got hold of a man, some Frenchman who had played a joke on her, perhaps because he had detected her English accent; anyway, it didn't really matter why. It had been a mistake, and by a considerable effort of will, still helped by the wine, he let himself be satisfied with this explanation, as if he were consciously setting aside hours of torture for himself in the near future; that very evening, for example, he would envisage all the other possibilities. In the meantime, he emptied his glass and even went so far as to contribute to the exchange of quips about adultery, and watched Ashley, who was making a parody of chatting up Georgia then Sue. After pudding John agreed to a glass of cognac and Georgia said: "I'll drive." He couldn't have said why, but this comment suddenly seemed rather vulgar and small-minded amongst all these people who were, anyway, drunk themselves too and had also accepted the offer of a glass of cognac. "I'll drive"; there was something petty and middle-class about it, when all was said and done. He had a second glass of cognac, then Ashley took them on a tour of the house. He took the opportunity to show Georgia the windows which needed curtains, but they decided that the measurements should be taken another day to be sure of getting them right. As they went through the guest bedrooms and admired the con-temporary paintings on the walls ("a magnificent collection," Joshua kept saying), John started to think about other explanations for the mysterious telephone call. There was only one: Georgia had a lover. Unless she had had friends to the house, a man and a woman for example, and she had gone out into the garden for a moment and the man in question had picked up the telephone while she was out and played his joke. But which man could it be? Dave could have come to have a cup of coffee with Helen. And Georgia hadn't mentioned it to him. Possible. But not very probable. Or it could have been a mistake. Yes, a mistake, of course. But every time he reached this conclusion, which was the most realistic of all, obscene, scatological images flitted through his mind for a fraction of a second and in amongst these silhou-ettes and blurred colours, in less time than it takes to tell, he could make out the pink outline created by Georgia's naked body and the other one with it, the body of this Frenchman because it had been a French voice, he was remembering now, a Frenchman, then... During the roast meat and gravy they had made enough comments and jokes about the art of lovemaking in France, and all that nonsense, and the Latin charm and God knows what else. And it had been a Frenchman, it couldn't have been Dave; why would Dave have picked up the telephone in their house? Even for a joke. And, anyway, Sue would have recognised his voice. Or maybe not? He hadn't detected any embarrassment on Georgia's part when Sue had told the story; even her surprise couldn't have been described as excessive, she hadn't blushed, she had only laughed with the others. He didn't dare smoke while they looked round the house, and he toyed nervously with the coins in his pocket, all those beds in the spare rooms made him want to lie down and go to sleep, high beds with deep, soft mattresses, fluffy eiderdowns and clean, fresh sheets. Then he turned away from the beds and looked out of the window at the grey rain and the transparent sky to avoid seeing those pink outlines which had suddenly reappeared before his eyes; in his imagination he could see the eiderdowns heaving up and down, the sheets crumpling. The admiring murmurings from Joshua and Sue, who already knew the place, deafened him. He looked at Georgia and thought she looked gorgeous, the make-up he had reproached her for so strictly that same morning aroused him now, made him want to be alone with her in one of these rooms, to lie down with her and – with what they did, with the touch of her skin and the smell of her body – he would erase all the furtive images that tortured him and that he couldn't control. He begged the high heavens for the questions to stop, to be cured of his jealousy, to be like the others. In the corridor when they got back down to the ground floor he went and walked alongside her. Joshua was talking to Ashley, and Sue was walking ahead. He would have liked to take her in his arms;

he looked for something to say, then just touched her arm lightly. She turned to look at him, he smiled and heard himself asking: "OK?" She frowned as if he had gone mad, then replied rather exasperatedly: "Yes, of course, why are you asking?" She talked quietly, afraid the others might hear, afraid that John's question might seem rude. Then she turned away and they continued their tour.

6

Old Desjean was leaning against a tree in the middle of the woods, hiding his face; his body convulsed regularly, he was crying and the tears streamed down his cheeks. He let himself slide down against the trunk and found himself sitting on the ground. He was close to Héloïse's house. He hadn't been able to stop himself coming back to see whether anything had changed, whether someone had come to the house, perhaps. He cried silently. He felt sorry for himself, and this was perhaps the first time since his childhood that he had so readily accommodated his own feelings and weaknesses. He took a big handkerchief out of his pocket. Then his astonishment suddenly dried up his tears. He sat, dumbstruck, staring into space, with an almost comical grimace on his face. He stood up and set off towards the house at a run.

He pushed the door open violently, as if he were expecting to see Héloïse and all the saints standing before him in the kitchen. She was still there, just where he had left her, her nostrils pinched, her neck thrown back. Her eyes and mouth open. And what about his knife? A shudder ran down his spine at the sight of this absurd dummy with his knife in its heart. He couldn't believe that he had left his knife in Héloïse's heart, even in the state of panic in which he had been two days earlier. He put his hand round the handle once again and pulled his Opinel out with one swift movement. No one had come. No one gave a damn about the poor old girl. He wondered whether he should set fire to the house. No, why draw attention to the place? Weeks might go past before anyone wondered what had happened to

Héloïse. Even the Pauillac parents wouldn't worry about her for a good while yet. The postman only went as far as the end of the track to put her mail in her box. Perhaps one day they would come to cut off the water supply. That wouldn't be for ages. He wondered whether he should close her eyes, or put her in her bed. No, obviously. But, all the same… Still, she was dead, after all. For the second time he abandoned her on the chair where he had stabbed her.

Sitting in his first-class compartment, John still had a hangover. He should never have agreed to go out for lunch the day before leaving for London. He had had more to drink when they came home from the lunch, and the cigarettes he was now smoking contributed to his feelings of nausea, but he couldn't help himself lighting them one after the other; every jolt of the train carrying him away to Limoges felt as if his stomach was being wrung out, and he found the acrid smell of the cigarettes, pipes and cigarillos of previous passengers intolerable – and he was the one who had always had a passion for tobacco. Opening the windows was out of the question, the day was as cold and grey as the façades of the square, stuccoed houses backing on to the railway line with their oversized windows and their iron bars. There was only one passenger opposite him, gazing out of the window, with his faded matinée idol looks, balding, greying, with thin, pursed lips, smoking Dunhills and sitting with his legs crossed in a rather precious way; his socks showed above his loafers with their snaffle link; they were rather worn, pointy shoes, obviously cheap. And between the slightly crinkled sock and the hem of his trousers there were a few black hairs standing out against the pale flesh, conjuring an image of his nakedness. John looked at him surreptitiously with shudders of disgust. He couldn't help thinking that this man must surely have slept with women, and everything about him exuded a sort of provincial lechery, the whiff of clandestine affairs, perhaps with a girl in the office, and of secret weekends in mediocre hotels, a leg-over after a greasy meal in an over-decorated restaurant.

He tried to immerse himself in his book again. In vain. His headache, the scenarios he was constructing around his fellow passenger, the metallic grinding of the very wheels, and the rattling of the windows, everything led him back to unpleasant thoughts. He tried to think about Ashley, or Sue. He didn't really know what to think about the lunch any more, even if Ashley did prove to be a useful contact, as they say. Maybe. He thought back to the comfortable, stress-free laziness that must set the rhythm to Ashley's life. He couldn't begin to imagine what sort of worries the man could have. Even his ugliness, his heavy eyelids and his puffy mouth counted for nothing beside his fortune.

Then, as if someone had whispered in his ear, one sentence rang out in his mind again, mingling with his nausea and his bitter feelings: "She's gone out, this is her cousin." A man's voice, a Frenchman, and such a ridiculous, comic sentence, worthy of one of those boulevard comedies the French seem to write – yes, the French, that was just it. The train was just drawing in to Bussière-Galant. He couldn't help smiling, this name (with its echoes of "gallant" and "bustier" or even "bush") so grotesquely summed up those stories of connecting bedroom doors and unmade beds with lovers hiding beneath them. The man opposite uncrossed his legs, coughed slightly and wriggled in his seat. And as the train gathered speed again, John's thoughts lost what little coherence they had had until then. "She's gone out, this is her cousin." It could only mean one thing: that Georgia had a French lover and, what's more, the man had had the good taste to take the mickey out of him, the poor cuckolded husband, by answering the telephone in his house – his, John's – to make a joke: "It's her cousin". Then the images came back to him, merciless as a migraine. Behind his closed eyelids he almost thought he could see the man opposite him in the compartment, sprawled over Georgia, their bodies intertwined, and her submitting to his every whim, and he would go on to tell all his friends about it, in great detail, as he leant against a bar, slowly getting drunk on pastis. John wanted to be sick. He went unsteadily to the toilets, bashing into the walls along the corridor. He opened the door, the stench was appalling, but he decided to splash some water over his face. He had started to sweat. He looked at himself in the mirror, thought he looked hideous, and could hardly recognise himself in this reflection. He frowned then dampened his brow. He was afraid he would remain in this state until it eventually killed him; he couldn't even envisage the next four days in London, talking about property, hectares and outbuildings, and all the while he would be wondering whether Georgia wasn't with a man at that very moment, giving herself to him in their bed with moans of pleasure. The train slowed down, he unlocked the door and went back out into the corridor. They were drawing in to a station. La Coquille. (Another ridiculous name, for goodness sake, it was both "cocky" and painfully close to the French for cuckold, "cocu"). He went into the compartment, pulled his suitcase from the metal rack and rushed to the door. The next minute he was out on the platform and the first thing he noticed was the fresh air on his face. He stood for a moment almost dumbstruck, contemplating the station building, then he heard the whistle blow and felt the train pulling out behind him. He looked over his shoulder with perfect indifference, as if he were no longer responsible for his actions. He made his way to the exit, now moving completely naturally, just like any other traveller who has reached their destination. He walked through a waiting-room that was more or less identical to the one he had left in Thiviers, and found himself outside. He looked about and felt he recognised this small-town landscape that he was actually seeing for the first time. There was a café opposite. He crossed the road, went in and sat at a table. While he carried out these unsurprising gestures his mind was a complete blank. A fat woman in an apron appeared behind the bar as she came out of the kitchen, followed by a German shepherd dog. John ordered a beer. It was hot in the café and the alcohol lulled him back into a pleasant torpor. He realised that he felt at peace. He was gradually overcome by a tremendous sense of freedom. No one knew he was there. No one knew he had done something he shouldn't have done. He had all the time in the world. He couldn't help himself smiling, it was as if he was suddenly back in control of his existence.

"Can I make a telephone call?" he asked the fat woman, who had stayed behind the bar and was leaning on it, watching the deserted street outside.

"Is it a local call?"

"No, abroad."

"Oh, in that case, no then, there are kiosks outside, look, in front of the station. If you've got a phone card…"

He waved his hand to show that it didn't matter, he would see to it later, and, to prove it to himself, he ordered another beer. The cigarettes tasted better now.

After half an hour he picked up his suitcase and went to ring the office in London. He could see La Coquille through the kiosk windows. The ringing sound alone at the other end of the line was enough to evoke England, London, the office; he could imagine in detail the snug reception area and that distinctive smell of paper, disinfectant and ink which was now familiar to him. He spoke to the receptionist for a while, letting her know that he was appallingly ill, that the doctor had been and had prescribed him all sorts of things that tasted appalling, but that he was hoping not to be in bed for more than two or three days. He spoke as if he were exhausted, almost like an impersonator, and he thought his own performance was utterly irresistible. Then he asked to speak to his boss.

"Martin?"

"John? How are you?"

"Not very well, in fact, that's why I'm calling."

"What's the matter?"

"Nothing serious. But I'm in bed. I've gone down with something."

A lorry went past along the road at this point, and he panicked for a moment before putting his hand over the mouthpiece to muffle the sound. Martin was silent, and he wondered whether he had heard the sound of the engine as the driver changed gear.

"Hello, Martin?"

"Yes."

"I can hardly hear you."

"Really? Well, listen, I don't know what to say. Look after yourself, old chap. Have you called the doctor?"

"Yes, yes. Georgia's been to get some medicine for me. It's nothing serious. But I'm completely drained."

"OK... I'm sorry to hear it."

(Why that tiny hesitation? Almost a note of incredulity in his voice. Someone had come up to the kiosk and was waiting to use the telephone. Please God he wouldn't open the door and ask for a light or something like that, or he didn't start shouting to a friend going into the café.)

"But if you like, Martin, if you really need me... you see, I've done some good work this week. I've made some useful contacts. I might be able to ask the doctor to give me something much stronger, so that I could take the train tonight, I don't know..."

"No, no, don't be ridiculous. No, what's one week. Stay in bed, whatever you do. You must shake this off."

(That was reassuring, he had done well to lay it on a bit, even if it initially comprised an element of risk.)

"Look, John, I'm going to have to leave you because I've got a meeting. But, as I said, look after yourself and come back when you're well enough. OK?"

"OK. Thanks, Martin."

"It's fine. OK, then, bye."

"Bye."

He hung up and burst out laughing. Couldn't have been easier. And they felt sorry for him. The person waiting, an adolescent in a tracksuit, with highlights in his hair that were totally incongruous in this rural setting, eyed him suspiciously. John, intoxicated by his success in the art of lying, wondered whether it would be as easy to kill someone like this unpleasant schoolboy as it was to justify your absence to your boss.

Georgia thought he was on his way to London. She must be thinking that she was free to do whatever she wanted for four days. In his present good mood, he thought that he might have judged her too harshly. But he still could not be sure of it. He wondered what she really did all day when he was away. He crossed back over the street, pushed the door to the café again and asked the *patronne*: "Are there any taxis here?"

"Hey, d'you know why curates are bald? Because when they're making love they kiss each other on the head." Louis roared with laughter as he reached the punch line of his joke, while old Desjean nodded and forced a smile. "Oh, I'm a stupid bugger!" cried Louis, taking one step back, two to the side and thumping Desjean's shoulder. They too were in a café, they had met outside the grocer's and had come in because that was what you did and, even if they didn't really feel like it, they had both gone in to have a Ricard. That was just the way it worked. It was half past nine in the morning.

"Ha, ha, and do you know this one? What did the Chinese girl say when the man tried to rape her? D'you know?"

He pointed his hooked, blackened finger under old Desjean's nose.

"No."

"Don't you know it?"

"No."

"She put her hands like this and said 'This is long, this is so long!' Get it? You know, wrong/long. I said I was a stupid bugger, didn't I?"

And the other man nodded in exactly the same way with exactly the same expression as after the first joke. Louis turned towards the *patron* and, still shouting, said: "Look, even he's laughing. Come on, are you having another one?"

Desjean shrugged and Louis concluded that this was an affirmative response. Young Desjean looked out of the window and sighed; he hadn't even bothered to pretend to laugh, he had stayed sitting at the table, slumped in his chair with something approaching arrogance in his attitude. As he fumbled through a wallet that was astonishingly small in relation to his great hands, Louis asked: "And that boy, there, is he having something?" knowing full well that his choice of words would prove prodigiously irritating to Jean Desjean. While he played the fool and bellowed at this relatively early hour, Louis was actually watching and trying to provoke a reaction. The father standing at the bar and the son sitting over by the window... there was something a bit strange about it.

"No thanks, not for me," replied Jean Desjean, aware that by refusing he was perhaps being almost insulting.

"Well!"

"No, I won't, 'cos after I'm going bye-byes," Jean added, imitating Louis's turn of phrase and adding a smile to compensate.

"Oh, I say! Oh, I say, listen to him! Have a Ricard, for goodness' sake!"

"Just a little one, then."

And Jean got up heavily to go for a pee. As he undid his flies he glanced at the calendars pinned to the walls. Australians and Americans sprawling on unmade beds, and showing off their tits and arses. He wondered, not for the first time, what it was his stepfather had done when he went into the English couple's house, and he didn't want to know what it was about these three or four pictures which had suddenly inspired the question. In the same way that he could never admit to himself why he had felt so angry when he realised that his stepfather had been in that woman's home. He told himself that no one had any right just going into good people's houses like that. And he stopped there with his explanations even though he was vaguely aware that that wasn't really it.

Making the most of Jean's absence, Louis turned to the older man and said: "How are things with you, then?"

"Still the same."

"The wife still on good form, is she?" he asked with a touch of rather forced innuendo.

The old man drank down his glass and gave no response. Sensing that he wouldn't get anywhere, Louis went on to talk about the cows he had bought at Saint-Yriex.

When Jean came back, he downed his glass in one, and the old boy slapped his hand down on the bar and said: "Right, we'd better get going, if we stay here much longer we'll be offered a job." And they headed for the door with Louis watching them all the way.

Old Desjean turned to Jean; then he thought of Louis but didn't dare look at him through the café window. A smile played on the corner of his lips. He had just been talking to a man whose sister he had killed, and he didn't even know. And the little prick next to him here, he didn't know either. He suddenly felt much less intimidated by either of them. He went on savouring this new situation as he drove his car, without saying a word to the younger man, and his sense of relief was not dissimilar to the kind of happiness he had felt after his first wife died; this feeling evolved into an idea…

Still in the café, Louis turned to Michel: "A couple of cheerful clowns, that pair. Specially the kid. Oh, my word."

"What d'you expect. They're just like that."

"Too right, they are."

Louis didn't feel sure enough of himself to press the matter any further at the moment and Marcellou had just come in, anyway.

"Marcellou, ho, Marcellou, ha, ha, hang on, d'you know this one? D'you know what the Chinese girl said when…"

It made Georgia jump when she heard footsteps behind her on the doorstep. She was still in her dressing gown. She instinctively brought her hand to her throat to close it more tightly.

"Did I frighten you? Are you all on your own?"

It was old Mother Pauillac. Georgia answered yes to both her questions and sighed. Then she felt slightly ashamed to be in this state, just out of bed, with her hair in a mess and sitting looking at her toast and her cup of tea, while she imagined that her neighbour had probably already done a full day's work. Old Mother Pauillac brandished a filthy old plastic bag covered in black marks that were difficult to identify but which suggested at least a mixture of mud and dust, then she announced: "I've brought you some eggs."

"Thank you, come in, sit down, would you like some coffee?"

(She had grasped that you didn't offer tea to the locals.)

"Oh…"

"It's nearly ready." And she went to make it, having put the eggs down on the table.

"If I could have the bag back..." Old Mme Pauillac asked shyly, a little embarrassed by her own pettiness, and then she added "So, has Monsieur John gone away?"

"Yes, this morning. I was tired, so I went back to bed when I got home," explained Georgia.

"You're not ill, are you?"

"No, no, I just... felt like it."

"It can't be much fun being all alone like this so often. When's your husband coming back?"

"In six days."

Sitting in the back of the taxi, John could see the counter was already over two hundred francs, and he was afraid he wouldn't have enough money to pay for the journey.

"Could we stop at a cash machine?" he asked the driver. "I need to take some money out."

"Whatever you say."

Luckily Georgia didn't inspect their bank statements too closely; she certainly would have been surprised to see that he had made a withdrawal for, say, four hundred francs on that particular day in Bussière-Galant or La Coquille or God knows where.

They were going through Thiviers; it was a tricky moment, he might be seen by someone who knew him. A shopkeeper who might mention it in front of Georgia: "You went past in a taxi the other day and I waved but you didn't see me." Not very likely. Anyway, he could always maintain that the imaginary shopkeeper had been wrong. As they came closer to the village and the countryside became as familiar as the inside of an apartment or a house he had lived in for a long time, with its smells, its imperfections and its furniture, boring because it has been there for so long, he started to feel uneasy, and the feeling that he shouldn't be there was now not as nice as it had been when he had been drinking his beer in La Coquille. After Saint-Jean-de-Côle he spoke to the driver again.

"Can you go left here? We'll go along the hill road and I'll get out at Tierchâteau."

"Whatever you say, but it's longer that way."

"It doesn't matter, I'd prefer that, I have to see someone in Tierchâteau."

The driver didn't ask for any more details, probably because his customer was English, that would go some way to explaining the fact that he had chosen to take a taxi for something approaching four hundred francs when he could have taken the train to Thiviers, and caught a taxi just for the last bit. Along the way they came across only one person, a local who had stopped his car to have a pee on the verge. The English know that it is difficult to take a country road in France without coming across someone who has stopped to do just that. But this particular one had his back to them and John didn't know him anyway. At Tierchâteau he paid the fare, telling the driver to keep the change and saying he would take his suitcase from the boot himself. As the tip was colossal, the driver insisted on getting the monsieur's luggage out, and the fact that he did it so slowly and deliberately was all the more exasperating for John because he had started to feel feverish with apprehension. When the car had disappeared round a bend, John jogged along, dragging his suitcase behind him. He couldn't see his house, but from Tierchâteau you could clearly make out the rooftops of the village where he and Georgia lived. He was too hot in his suit and his raincoat, and he needed to think. To his right a field of maize stretched along the sideroad to Villars, and on to the junction with another road which was so full of bumps and ruts that it was little more than a track.

He covered some thirty metres and then, there amongst the young maize plants, as if he were lost in some rustic jungle, he took off his raincoat and loosened his tie.

She was still there, as if she were waiting for him. Stiff. The only difference lay in the repulsive smell which must have been due to the life that continued to burgeon within her, transforming her. He had never seen a five-day-old corpse. Apart from animals, of course. There she was, Héloïse, in the beam of his torch. He was careful not to switch the light on. It was dark outside. Old Desjean had thought at length, deliberated with himself, now that he was calm again and the tears were behind him. He had wondered whether he should tackle the English girl and her husband first, then he had decided that they could wait and he would start with Louis. The police and their experts would be able to tell that the 'victim' – as they said – had been dead for five days. But that wouldn't matter. It would be up to Louis to sort himself out and prove his innocence, he would certainly rant and shout about that... And Desjean couldn't help smiling. Lighting up the floor with his torch, he moved closer to the body with something akin to regret and, as he had done so many times before, he took Héloïse in his arms.

After spending half an hour in the middle of his field of maize, sitting on his suitcase, John suddenly recognised the white outline of his own car going up the hill towards Saint-Pierre. It was the third car he had seen. Each time he was afraid of being spotted because of his grey suit, which must have stood out against the field like a scarecrow's rags. But this time, he was quite sure of it, Georgia had set off in the car to go shopping (but why Saint-

Pierre? She usually went to Thiviers via Saint-Jean-de-Côle). He didn't have time to find an answer to his questions, they could gnaw away at him later. For now, he grabbed his suitcase and fled as quickly as the maize would allow. He was bathed in sweat by the time he reached the road. The weight of the suitcase was giving him cramps in his upper arm. He crossed the road with furtive backward glances like someone who thinks they are being followed in the middle of a big city. He went into the woods and after just a few paces he decided to abandon his suitcase, thinking he could come back for it later, at night, perhaps. He started to run, his shoes slipping on the fallen leaves and his flapping raincoat snagging on branches and brambles. He decided to make a long detour so as to avoid the open fields. The fear that gripped him prevented him from realising that he had no particular plan of action. In his haste, he had forgotten to look at his watch to gauge how much time he had at his disposal before Georgia came back. No errand would take less than twenty minutes. He tried to evaluate how much time he had just spent panicking and achieving precious little. Impossible. He heard the sound of a wheezy, lumbering engine. A tractor. He couldn't see it between the trees. He ran his hand through his hair, stroked the back of his neck and gave a long sigh. This despondency lasted all of three seconds before he set off again. Sometimes he took great purposeful strides without really knowing why, merely following the erratic rhythm of his own anxieties. As he came out of the woods he didn't immediately recognise the building that stood ahead of him on the far side of the field where Louis kept his horses. A huge wall blocked his view, and it was interrupted by only one small entrance where a faded, green door hung precariously on its hinges. He suddenly realised that this was the barn just opposite his house. He bent over to slip under the electric fence and walked slowly so as not to disturb the horses, a mare with her foal and a massive stallion. They looked up at him indifferently before going back to their grazing. He had no trouble at all pushing open the door and slipping into the darkness inside the barn. He stood absolutely motionless and watched the daylight through a rectangular window which punctuated the other side of the barn on the ground floor. The ground was carpeted in horse dung, and his English brogues sank into it as he made his way to the wooden ladder up to the first floor. From there he could see his house and his bedroom window through the other window which he had seen as a big black square every morning, without ever really paying it much attention. He finally let himself fall down on to the straw, staring up at the maze of beams overhead. Then he heard an engine sound, a car this time, slowing down and stopping. It was not a familiar sound.

They weren't there. Their white Peugeot estate wasn't in the yard where it was usually parked. He was tempted to get out, to walk some way across the yard. The dog hadn't barked. What if they came back? Perhaps she would be on her own. So what? Not much point in delving round here again. "She's gone out. I'm her cousin." He was still laughing about it. Even though he didn't know what had persuaded him to pick up the telephone when he had been to their house that first time. It was as if all the ghosts he had seen round the fireplace had made him do it. Then he had left and that was where the memory became less pleasing. The little bastard had caught him at it. He wondered where on earth he could have put himself to have seen him without being seen. Unless, not for the first time, he had been told. But who? Perhaps that bugger Louis. He was watching him too, he could feel it. But Louis still wasn't careful enough. There was a surprise waiting for him… the game was becoming dangerous. But, what the hell? When Desjean was on his own, he could still laugh about it.

★

Lying in the straw, John had not been able to see who was driving the blue Renault 4. The skylight in the barn was too far up for him to see the inside of the car, and he had to be careful to stay in the shadows. As the car went off down the road before it disappeared, he heard the telephone ringing in his house, long calls that were in turns plangent and menacing, and that went unanswered. What if it was the office ringing back for news of him? And they would be amazed that there was nobody there. No, it was still too soon. It was only a few hours since he had told them he was ill. If it was one of their friends they would be calling Georgia because they all knew that he was in London. His heart constricted as he listened to the ringing: even though he didn't really know why he found the regular, strident sound stressful. Just Helen or Sue Brimmington-Smythe wanting to come over for a cup of tea and a gossip.

Then it fell silent. He stayed there listening to the rustling of the leaves, keeping an eye out for any movement in the straw, wondering whether Louis would come to use the barn or to look for one of the tools he kept down below. After an hour spent waiting like this, he started to feel bored; he almost went so far as to want some dramatic event to happen. The cold seeped into him and he looked at his creased suit, covered in dust and straw. There was no possible episode in his London life which could justify the state of his clothes when he "came home" in four days' time, wearied by the pace of the city, welcomed gratefully by a loving wife because he was sacrificing his rustic happiness to bring home his salary for which he toiled until exhausted. He thought that he was going to have to go into the house in the next couple of days – while Georgia was out because she was bound to need to go and buy something – to take some more appropriate clothes, then he would go and pick up his suitcase in the woods and would change on the day he was meant to be getting back. Unless, of course, he caught her cheating on him, then he wouldn't have to justify anything. He wanted a cigarette and he wondered whether it was a good idea in the middle of all this dried grass; he decided to forego it. He didn't dare venture down the ladder where it would not have been so dangerous, just so that he could smoke. He looked at his watch, he had now been in the barn for just over an hour and, as he was beginning to get used to this extraordinary situation, he began to succumb to boredom, swiftly followed by hunger. His fridge was there just across the track, and there was still some cheese and butter in it; he wondered whether there was any bread, and he would have gladly taken some cereal from the larder cupboard. He was seized with panic as he wondered how he was going to last for four days without food, then he decided that he would steal some from home as soon as Georgia went out. That was when he heard the sound of his car engine and the crunch of tyres as she braked. He went over to the window, still lying down on his tummy, and watched Georgia opening the door to let out the dog, which started running in circles and jumping up at her. The dog! Would the dog be able to smell him from here? No, but what if he left his hiding place? For now, there was apparently nothing to fear. Georgia opened the boot and took out some supermarket bags, and – watching her like this, unseen, seeing and recognising her every move – he felt a surge of tenderness towards her, he was moved to see her alone at this farmhouse lost in the middle of France with her dog as her only companion, waiting day after day for him to come back from London. His own feelings managed to reassure him about the state of their marriage. He noticed that she really was taking an awful lot of bags of food out of that boot, and that he could hear lots of bottles clinking too. Perhaps she always did her week's shopping the day he left. Still prey to the affection he had just felt, he hoped that to pass the time in his absence she wasn't drinking too much.

★

Louis was getting fed up with having to spend every evening drinking with these losers in order to buy and sell livestock. He didn't have a watch, he boasted about the fact often enough, but he knew that it must be about three o'clock in the morning. He had been ambushed in his local, then he had had to drop in on a client where he waited for the pastis to polish him off before heading home. The dogs were barking furiously in their kennel and he knew the neighbours would have a go at him again in the morning. He started to push his cap back but stopped the familiar gesture short. There was a silhouette slumped in front of his door, lit by the blue-white light of the moon. At first he thought that it was a friend who was blind drunk and had collapsed on his doorstep when he found no one at home. He swore and took a few steps before stopping. He recognised his sister's face but he needed to be sure. Her cheeks were marbled blue and yellow with patches of purple here and there, her mouth was open to reveal her toothless gums, her black hair was loose, falling over her shoulders like old pieces of string, shreds of black fabric. And he realised that she was dead. He leant backwards and puffed out his chest to ward off any normal sort of reaction: panic, incomprehension, sorrow. He shone his torch on the body and saw that there were splashes of dried blood on her dress. From time to time a breath of air would lift a few strands of hair, giving the body a semblance of life. Louis shone his torch on the face, saw the open eyes and was frightened.

He turned round, the farmyard was empty. Then he realised that, the whole time he had been there, the dogs had been barking at him. He was tempted to shout at them to shut them up. Then he decided it would be better not to make any noise. He went over to the kennel, opened the gate to their run and stroked the dogs to calm them down before feeding them. He went back over to the body and, despite his revulsion, he lifted the dress where it was stained with blood. He could see straight away that the wound had been made by a sharp object. A knife. The corpse stank, but he was used to that. Louis took his head in his hands, looked at the farmyard again, then decided that the first thing he must do was to hide the body. He grabbed it by the feet and, while he dragged it over to the barn, he wondered who had killed Héloïse and why. He quickly came to the conclusion that she had been killed somewhere else and had been brought to his door. As a threat? Perhaps. Plenty of people didn't like him, but he couldn't think of anyone who hated him enough to kill his sister and bring her all the way to him. What if someone else had found the body? He would have been blamed. And then what?

In the barn he could see the forklift attachment on his tractor standing out clearly against the darkness like a gallows. He took a rope and attached one end to one of Héloïse's ankles and the other to one of the prongs of the fork. He lifted the body, which hung down, still slightly stiff. With its hair dragging on the ground and its mouth still open, it looked like a primitive statue for some monstrous cult. Then he drove his tractor, making an infernal racket, to the nearest ploughed field. If he met anyone he had had it, for sure. He could see the moon sinking lower in the sky and emitting an alarming amount of light. The body swung from left to right in front of him. This was the only thing he could do. To bury Héloïse secretly and to find out for himself who had killed her. But then... he would tell his mother that his bitch of a sister had gone off somewhere with one of her lovers without a word to anyone. Angoulême or somewhere. Why not Paris. As he thought things through, he thought there was something missing in this drunkard's nightmare which had proved to be an undeniable reality and which he had assimilated and mastered with a speed that amazed even himself. Then he realised what was lacking. His pain. He didn't feel any sorrow for this sister he had lost so long ago. Had never had, in fact.

He decided to bury her in the middle of the field. No one would come to plough there except for him, and he easily dug a deep hole. The soil was soft, rich and heavy here, and for once not too stony. He had buried more than one dog like this in the past.

After the boredom and the hunger came the cold. Georgia had unloaded the car and had disappeared into the house. John had not seen her all day, and night was beginning to fall, a new nuance of grey was slowly invading the sky, there were different sounds, it felt as if the day's activities were drawing to a close, he could hear the Pauillacs closing their gates. The coolness in the air made him want to be sitting by a fire, glass in hand, or in a restaurant in London. Could he leave the barn, cut across the twenty or thirty metres that separated him from his wife and tell her... tell her what exactly, that he had spent the day in the straw instead of going to work in England? He couldn't really believe it himself. The light went on in his bedroom. He stretched his neck but Georgia didn't walk past the window, and he would have so liked to have seen her, just for a moment. He went back to his train of thought, and decided that he would set out in the night to get his suitcase, he would put a sweater on, no... he had to keep some clean clothes for when he came home, so he would go on living in his suit and at the last minute he would get rid of it and say that he had left it with a dry cleaner in London because he had spilled wine on it during a lunch with a client, for example. Perfect. Or that the client had spilled the bottle over him, better still. All the same, four days like this. An eternity. He burrowed a hole in the straw in preparation for the night, and after an hour of ruminating on thoughts that went round in circles and escalated in a series of deafening echoes, he heard an engine sound again, then he saw headlights sweeping round the yard in front of the house before going out. Two doors slamming, and he suddenly made out Helen's silhouette, then Dave's, holding a bottle of wine and turning to say something John couldn't hear to Helen, and the two of them laughing. John watches as they cross the yard, he sees the door open, but he still can't see his wife; she must be waving them in, everyone disappears, the door closes. He can now see why she unloaded so many bags and so much wine earlier. At least she isn't wasting any time consoling herself while he's away, not hanging about to have a good time, and the rest of the night he would spend in a state of outraged indignation.

In spite of his anger, he eventually went to sleep, lying under his raincoat which he had covered with straw. He was woken by the sound of the door opening, Helen and Dave's slightly hoarse voices and Georgia's laugh; she was holding a torch but was clearly silhouetted against the light coming from the open door. They are all drunk and he even catches himself thinking them rather ridiculous. Georgia's laugh sounds hysterical to him. Helen helps Dave to the car, and he turns round to make one last quip. Then John can see Georgia waving to them in the beam of the headlights. He notices that she has changed, she was wearing a dress, that's what she was doing in the bedroom earlier. When he's there, she never changes when they have friends to supper. But surely she can't be trying to seduce her best friend's partner? The door closes again with a clamour of wood and glass. Thereafter he can follow her movements as the lights go on and off: she has gone up to bed. She opens the wardrobe, she takes off her dress and, in the mirror on the inside of the wardrobe door, he can see her take off her bra and then her knickers. Before her reflection disappears as she slips between the sheets, she puts on a T-shirt. He wonders whether at any time anyone else has watched her like this from this barn, ogling her, looking at her naked body, and he starts to loathe this imaginary voyeur.

7

Louis walked silently through the undergrowth, his footsteps deadened by the fallen leaves, he just had to be careful not to snap any twigs. He watched the dog sniffing the ground in front of him and zigzagging at dizzying speed, then the animal stopped and bent back one paw as if he were indicating a pheasant or a partridge. Louis closed his gun. He knew he was too close to the road and even to inhabited houses, he would have liked to be out in the open and to have let the dog do his work. The animal was like a statue, standing a little ahead of him, with its nose pointing and its tail rigid. Louis shouldered his gun and spoke quietly to the dog: "Flush it out!" The dog put its paw back down and moved forward, wagging its tail and sniffing a square-shaped object. Louis lowered his gun and started muttering ("piece of shit", "pointer, my arse", "you watch it, mate, or I'll see to you", etc.) when he saw that the dog had found an old suitcase. Furious, he gave it a good kick, and then he realised that it wasn't as old as all that. He bent over it, breathing heavily, brushed off the dead leaves and opened it without any trouble. Inside he found a whole collection of shirts which had been carefully ironed and folded, good quality shirts, or at least they looked so to him, a pair of suit trousers, a muddle of socks and a washbag. "Well, what have we here?" he said out loud, then under the shirts he found a sweater which was somehow familiar to him. It was clear that the clothes weren't new, they had been worn by a man, ironed and folded by his wife, the whole layout of this piece of luggage represented years of communal life, of habits and intimacy, an intimacy that he almost felt he was violating as he ran his muddy hands over the spotless collars and cuffs. Like going into the bathroom of someone you hardly know. He felt an almost irrational anxiety at finding these clothes in the undergrowth, but he kept trying to remember where he had seen that sweater before. He frowned and looked up to the tops of the trees as if for inspiration, and eventually an image of the Englishman came to mind. He could picture him with his hands in his pockets, his shoulders back and his nose in the air, walking through Thiviers, wearing this sweater. What the hell was it doing here now? You don't just lose a suitcase in the woods, someone must have chucked it here. Who? Why? Thieves? He wondered whether there was any link between this discovery and his sister's death. Whether it was the Englishman who had wanted to kill her and to put the blame on him. Why? He couldn't find an answer to that question. All the same he had a vague feeling that there was some connection between this suitcase, the English couple and Héloïse. He felt frightened for them. He thought that he must find whoever killed Héloïse in order to protect these good people. Then he felt as if a weight had suddenly been lowered on to his shoulders as he wondered whether the Englishman was in fact still alive himself.

Two gunshots in quick succession and John opened his eyes, still lying down in the straw. As he took in the black beams overhead and saw the cold, fragile light of dawn creeping in feebly he understood that people were out shooting close by. Wednesday. On the morning of the previous day his life had still been normal, or almost. Today he was waking up in his suit in the barn opposite his house, and no one knew he was there. He rolled on to his front to look at his bedroom window and to check his watch. Seven o'clock. Georgia was still asleep. He felt a moment of affection mingled with desire as he imagined her sleeping face on the pillow, her blond hair forming waves in the folds of the fabric. Then he remembered that she would be nursing a hangover from the night before when she had made the most of his absence to enjoy herself. He still thought he felt surprisingly fresh despite the terrible conditions in which he had spent the night, and concluded that it must have been because he hadn't had anything to drink the night before. He tried to devise a programme for himself for the day even though he knew full well that any such plan was downright ridiculous. He had trouble assessing his own feelings. In some ways he was happy not to be in London singing the praises of properties he would never be able to afford to people he would never be able to abide. When all was said and done, his situation didn't really surprise him that much; on the contrary, what really surprised him was how easily he had come to accept it as his new form of normality. So, he was going to pick up his suitcase but not before nightfall because the woods were teaming with men out shooting; he was going to go into his own house while Georgia was out to steal some food, sardines in the utility area that the locals insisted on calling a cellar; he would take a book, a thick novel which would help to pass the time, perhaps a bottle of wine too. While he made his shopping list he gazed admiringly at the morning sunlight. At ten o'clock, three hours after he woke up, he could still see no signs of life in the house, Georgia was still asleep. She was certainly doing as she pleased. She obviously had bugger all to do with her days, because at this point John could almost convince himself that he was slaving away in London. In any event, even if he knew it wasn't true, she should have been quite sure that it was.

At eleven o'clock he heard her open the kitchen door, although he couldn't actually see her. He was dying of hunger. She would almost definitely be in her dressing gown, making some toast. He could see the dog bounding in the courtyard and stopping by the barn wall to lift his leg. God, he was patient. He must have been holding it in all this time, waiting for her to open the door for him. Now that he was in this frame of mind, John remembered a few episodes in their life together which he had found prodigiously irritating and, taut with annoyance, he got into position like a sniper to wait for the arrival of the lover who now seemed to him to be an inescapable certainty.

It was only when he was on the road at the wheel of his car that Louis thought he might have been wrong to take the suitcase, and that if the Englishman were dead it would seem even more strange for his belongings to be in his possession. He thought about going to see the Englishwoman to give her back the shirts, socks and underwear, and to ask her what was going on. But there again, what would people say? And he couldn't go and put it back where he had found it, either. He was driving without paying much attention to the traffic (a total of two cars) coming towards him. He had no one to talk to. Louis was alone. And, anyway, you didn't confide to a horse dealer, so much so that he was a bit wary himself even if he did spend his time telling stupid stories which he nevertheless found amusing. And one phrase kept coming back to him like a refrain from a hackneyed song, like an incantation: "They're good people, they are." And yet he would have found it difficult to explain why he felt this affection for them; it was something he no longer felt for the locals, he had seen too much of them, and he himself was unaware of the fact that he was too full of life, drive and ambition for this cramped place. He felt it intuitively, though, and he hesitated to admit it to himself.

Georgia decided that she wouldn't go out at all that day. She was annoyed with herself for getting drunk the night before and she put two soluble aspirins into a Pyrex glass, drinking it in little sips as if it were a cocktail while she buttered her toast. It was a chilly but beautiful day and she persuaded herself that autumn weather like this never happened in England. She thought she would have a shower and might go back to bed to get over her headache. She switched on the radio and listened to some soothing burblings about genetic modification. If anyone had asked what this particular programme on Radio 4 was about she wouldn't have been able to say, but she occasionally recognised the odd word which held her attention for a second or so between two mouthfuls of toast.

John didn't see her all day; she didn't take the dog for a walk, a setter, for goodness' sake, an animal that needed to run and let off steam for hours on end. He wouldn't even be able to have a go at her about it when he got back because he wasn't supposed to know. Starving, he climbed down the ladder and stood on the ground floor. He found a bag of horse nuts. He took one and tasted it, telling himself it was just dried grass and that he had been happy enough eating seaweed in the Japanese restaurant he had been taken to by some clients who owned a loft and had been watching their figures. The Japanese restaurant was better, though, and he spat out his horse nuts. There was also an open sack of barley left there by Louis. The result was more or less the same. He was so desperate to smoke that he would have accepted crack if he had been offered it, and he decided that as soon as night fell he would go out to the back of the barn and light a cigarette. At midday, as there was nothing but non-flammable horse dung underfoot on the ground floor, he gave in to temptation, still staying on his guard in case Louis came to bring in his horses or to look for one of the tools that lived there and which he, John, examined to pass the time: a crowbar, a sledge-hammer which weighed at least seven kilos, a pickaxe with a broken handle and an old wooden rake like the ones that they varnish and attach to the ceiling in provincial restaurants. His inspection of the tools had lasted six minutes.

Still nothing. That fat idiot Louis was still going round shouting from one café to the next and from one village to the next, and no one was talking about Héloïse's death. No one had found the body. Except perhaps for Louis himself. And in that case... in that case what? Had he burned the body? On the open fire? In the wood-burner? Old Desjean watched Jean, who was turned towards the window as he drank his soup. And his wife, who wasn't saying anything. No one was saying anything. He couldn't take it any more, he needed noise, policemen, screams. He wondered whether he had made a mistake. Louis couldn't have hidden Héloïse's body like that. He always got up later than his neighbour. He went to bed at about eleven and sometimes even midnight. And that was way too late for a man of the land. He might have gone out for a piss in the middle of the night. No, he had a toilet in the house. Like everyone else. This wasn't the old days any longer. He thought about his parents' house for a moment, giving himself a brief respite in spite of himself.

"Aren't you hungry?"

It was the wife who had spoken. And the boy had looked up, eyed his still full bowl of yellowish soup with the big hunk of bread from the day before and the pasta threads floating in the middle. He must have thought it was strange. Old Desjean forced himself to swallow a spoonful to avoid attracting attention from his wife and stepson.

"You're not ill, are you?"

"No."

"What is it, then?"

"Nothing."

"But…"

"Nothing, I said, for God's sake."

And he got up and went out without really knowing what he was going to do. He went over to his Renault 4, sat at the wheel and set off.

He decided to park in a space set aside for shooting, a little way from the road. And to cover the rest of the way on foot, cutting through the woods.

It was further than he had thought. It was a good quarter of an hour before he caught sight of the house. His heart felt heavy when he saw the window with the checked curtains and just behind them the vase full of dirty water still holding the stem of a flower that had long since wilted. He was completely mad to come back, he fully realised that, but he could no longer think straight. He almost expected the body to be there still, on her chair. And yet he had taken it away himself. But he was frightened, that was all. He picked up the chair that he had knocked over during his last visit and which he had left like that when he was weighed down with his mistress's inert body. He conscientiously put it back at the end of the table. He walked carefully, although he didn't really know why, and he ran his fingers over things as he came to them: the plates on which he had eaten with Héloïse, the glasses. He looked at the bottle of *pineau* in its place, still half full. Then the bed with its nylon cover. Then the circle of lace under the blue opaline lamp on the bedside table. The television on its little formica-covered sideboard, the old fridge with its patches of rust in the corners. It was like an album of old photographs or the remains of a good, enjoyable meal when you come across them the following morning after everyone has left. It made him forget the fear that had driven him back to this house. He was beginning to realise that he missed Héloïse.

★

The days were drawing in considerably and Georgia felt it all the more keenly because she settled herself at the sewing machine in the middle of the afternoon, minutely organising her pins, her lengths of cloth and her reels of thread, which between them created a whole world to which Radio 4 lent its English voice. That was her evening ritual. It was dark in the kitchen and she felt despondent for a moment; it was as if the sun never really rose. Or it did for just long enough for her to take on board the fact that she had a headache and she was alone. The dog, which whirled round her begging for his walk, had ended up irritating her; when he put his front paws on her knees, she pushed him away impatiently.

Impatience and the feeling that the days were getting shorter, that was what John was experiencing at the time too. But nightfall was a relief. He had only three cigarettes left. He had obviously intended to buy more in London, or even in Paris when he changed trains, and where he was now there was nothing else to do but smoke. He had calculated that it would be best to go and get his suitcase, which had his book in it, towards eight or nine o'clock, when everyone would be eating and it would be dark. Just one more hour to wait. He allowed himself a cigarette.

Old Desjean for his part had gone for a drink after leaving Héloïse's house. He was the only person in the bar, and that was no bad thing. He had had one Ricard, then another, then a third. He was holding up well. He looked at his watch. Eight o'clock. The boy would already be under his mother's skirts waiting for his supper. Desjean didn't feel like going home. The *patron* wasn't paying him any attention. He had his back to him and was leaning, one hand on the bar, with his cloth over his shoulder, watching a soap opera on the television suspended in the corner of the room, just under the ceiling and next to a playmate from *Playboy* or *Penthouse*, and a shelf unit with a selection of trophies which had been brought back from various places but no one could remember why any longer. He decided, or rather the Ricard decided for him, that he would make a courtesy call on the Pauillacs. Just like that. To see whether they'd finally had some news of their daughter, for example. Héloïse. He was on to his ninth Ricard.

He walked backwards, missing the wall by one of those miracles so common to drunkards, which considerably prolong their existence. His headlights swept through the undergrowth at every turn. But it wasn't that far, he only had to go along the hill for about a kilometre and he would come to the plateau where the little village stood. The bracken and the branches took on strange shapes under the effects of his tiredness and the alcohol; the puddles sometimes reflected an eerie yellow light. It had started to rain, a veil of drizzle sprinkling pearly droplets on the windscreen and distorting still further everything that the woods kept half hidden.

Suddenly he braked sharply, smacking his forehead on to the steering wheel and cursing. The windscreen wipers swept maddeningly across his field of vision. He leant forward and tried to make out whatever it was that had just appeared to him and was now no longer there. The silhouette of a man in a smart raincoat, running awkwardly and slipping, there one minute and gone the next. He turned to the right and thought he could still see this person, a reasonably tall figure, melting into a tree trunk. A shoulder, a suggestion of a profile, nothing more. And yet... a split second later there was nothing but the woodland around him. He had to admit that he was a little drunk. He shuddered as he wondered who could be hunting him down. He sat rooted to the spot as he appreciated the sheer amplitude of his fear. He set off again and, just a hundred metres further on, turned into the Pauillacs' courtyard.

John lay on the ground on the damp earth. He was gasping, with his mouth wide open and his face barely a few centimetres from the carpet of dead leaves, reddened bracken and pine needles drowned by the darkness. He had only that one field to cross, and a car just had to come along at that precise moment. The man must have seen him because he had stopped. It remained to be seen whether he had recognised him. The car set off again very soon afterwards. It had disappeared behind the barn that belonged to the two "cousins", and he hadn't seen it come out on to the road to Saint-Pierre on the far side of the village. Several explanations offered themselves. The driver had gone to the Pauillacs'. Or to his house. He had gone to see Georgia. Her lover? He clenched his teeth and his fists, then he held his head in his hands and was tempted to cry there and then on the dead leaves about his unhappy fate, about the cold and about Georgia.

He leapt back to his feet and ran back towards his house, hesitating briefly in the middle of the field. And what if it wasn't Georgia's lover, and what if she happened to come out at this exact moment and saw him like this? He hadn't seen himself in a mirror for more than twenty-four hours, but he had no trouble imagining that he looked like something not unrelated to a werewolf, with his stubble, the filth on his suit and his unbrushed hair full of straw. He set off again, running all the faster. He ran round the barn, went in through the door at the back and went back up to the first floor. There was only his car in front of the house. He heaved a great sigh. He didn't know what was more depressing. Spending the night in his soaking wet clothes and possibly having to wait another whole day or tackling this night commando course to get his suitcase. He stayed where he was, lying on his back in the straw, feeling the drops of water running between his shoulder blades. Then he got up and went back over to the ladder.

As soon as he came in, having knocked on the door but not waited for a reply, the Pauillacs could see that Desjean was drunk.

"Well, hello," called old man Pauillac after a marked pause and in a rather forced tone, as he invited him to sit down, pulling up a chair noisily.

The intruder sat down and was about to reply when he saw that the Englishwoman was sitting there with the Pauillacs. He opened his mouth then smiled slowly; it was almost a grimace and the alcohol gave it a lewd slant. She turned her eyes on to Madame Pauillac as if asking for help. The latter was wiping her hands on her cloth, and she looked from Desjean to her husband and then to Georgia.

"So, you've got visitors," said Desjean.

"As you can see. It's evening, isn't it. What about you? Aren't you at home eating at a time like this?" asked old man Pauillac, passing off this comment as a rather brusque joke.

Desjean was too addled by the Ricard to find an appropriate answer. He shrugged his shoulders and asked: "So, are you not offering me a Ricard then?"

"It doesn't look as if it's the first you've been offered," said Mother Pauillac, pouring one all the same.

"This is our neighbour, Madame Georgia," said old man Pauillac, picking up the etiquette where it had been left off.

"But we know each other, don't we, because we've already met here."

"Oh, that's right," old Mother Pauillac rallied with false lightness. "And Monsieur John was here then too."

"And where is he now?" asked Desjean.

"He's gone off to work, to London, in England. He works there every month, in real estate, doesn't he, Georgia? So we've asked our neighbour over for supper, as you can see," concluded old man Pauillac, indicating their plates full of food which no one had touched since Desjean came in.

Old Mother Pauillac shot a look at her husband. He noticed, but didn't realise that it was because he had said too much.

"Oh, now that can't be much fun, being all alone like that," said Desjean with what was meant to be a paternal note in his voice but it somehow sounded obscene. "When's he coming back?"

"The day after tomorrow."

Georgia hadn't had any other choice than to reply. Perhaps she should have said tomorrow. She hadn't given herself time to think. And even if she had never liked this character, she couldn't see any reason to be unduly wary of him.

"Does your wife know you're here?" asked old man Pauillac, who could guess the answer.

Desjean gave a groan, which he accompanied with a shrug of his shoulders. He still hadn't touched the glass that had been put in front of him.

"Dear me, are you going to go home in this state?" asked Mother Pauillac.

"What's it to you, then?"

He looked from his hands up to Georgia, and his gaze lingered on her breasts. She looked down, and sat there neatly with her hands crossed on her knees. Old Desjean wobbled his head from time to time. No one knew why. Even the old dog curled in its basket next to the cooker eyed him with a degree of disgust. Perhaps because he had met the animal's eye, he suddenly picked up his glass and downed it in one as he got to his feet.

"Right then!"

This was by way of saying that he had faced the facts and that, given he wasn't welcome... Almost a threat.

"Thank you for the Ricard. But, you know, keep an eye out all the same. D'you know, on the way here I saw someone running across the field in the rain. There are people on the prowl, so…"

He tried to finish his sentence but couldn't find anything better to say than just "keep an eye out" again, because that was what best translated his thoughts. Then he walked out of the door, and the dog finally started to bark.

"Shall I pour you some more wine, Madame Georgia?" asked old man Pauillac.

Was it an illusion or was the rain falling harder than on his first excursion? He had crossed the field without any hindrance this time and he was feeling his way through the woods from one tree to the next, looking for his suitcase. He twisted his ankle every three steps and had to stop himself from crying out in pain and surprise. Branches snapped under his feet, but the constant trickling of the raindrops through the trees as they fell from one leaf to the next must have covered these noises easily. He couldn't see a thing. Not a thing. The sky only just looked slightly greyer than the woods. He lit his lighter which made a globe of yellow light with a circumference of about five centimetres. When this feeble glow allowed him to distinguish vaguely the outline of a couple of fronds of bracken he burned his fingers, and he decided to turn back.

The straw in the barn seemed almost comfortable after the woods. He heard footsteps. A rhythm he would recognise in a thousand. He went over to the window and saw Georgia's silhouette. What was she doing there? He hadn't even seen her going out. She must have gone out for a walk the first time he set out for the woods. His back turned to ice at the thought that she could have seen him. So much so that he had difficulty breathing. Out for a walk at this time of night? She'd gone mad. He was shivering with cold. Once she was inside the house, he climbed down the ladder and looked for something to use as a cover. He eventually found some plastic sheeting covering a complicated piece of agricultural equipment designed to do he couldn't imagine what. That would do. He pulled this huge piece of black plastic up the ladder behind him like a giant bat going back to find its favourite beam to hang from. He also took a handful of barley and chewed on it for hours. If only he could have found a cob of raw maize, he would have nibbled on it with indescribable delight like a pig in its trough. Then he went to sleep like a new-born babe there in the depths of his stable.

Desjean was also sleeping soundly that night, producing deep, noisy guttural snores which earned him at least three jabs with an elbow between the shoulder blades during the course of the night. He didn't dream, and was woken by the noise that his wife and Jean were making in the kitchen. The nauseating noises of early morning, all that fussing around chipped bowls, the same ones they had been using for years, slices of bread and the jam that had too much sugar in it, the same gestures and the same words. He sat on the edge of the bed and felt as if he were on a boat in the middle of a storm. A new experience for this Périgordian, who had seen the sea possibly twice in his life. He put on his clothes without washing. The effort he put into putting on his socks and his vest prevented him from thinking. He thrust his hand into the pocket of his faded blue trousers and checked that his knife hadn't fallen out. Once he was reassured of this he thought of the events of the previous day and shook his head, despite the pain this inflicted on him. What on earth had persuaded him to go to the Pauillacs' in such a state after what he had done? He was overcome with terrible shame which he managed to eradicate with a painful smile. And that blonde had been there. The one who lived in his house, his. Then he thought about what old man Pauillac had said. That the husband went off for weeks at a time, to England, to London. He got to his feet, pushing himself up from the bedpost, then took a few steps over to the door. He could hear the mother and son talking below, but he couldn't make out their words.

Jean was the first to see his legs as they appeared down the stairs.

"You were in a pretty state last night. I could hear you bumping into all the walls."

"Jean!" said his mother rather limply, secretly pleased that someone had taken responsibility for reprimanding her husband for his drunkenness.

Old Desjean made his way over to the kitchen sink and put his head under a stream of cold water.

"Not in the kitchen," said his wife, still just as limply. "In the bathroom!"

One of the things that Desjean had kept from his childhood was a deep mistrust of bathrooms and hot water tanks, not to mention bath towels. He had been forced to give in because she had insisted on it, and they had given that bastard Favre a fortune to install the thing, because she was determined to use a professional and had refused his suggestion that he could do it all himself to save money.

"Where were you then?" asked Jean in the same aggressive tone.

"Hey!"

"Can't you tell us?"

"I went for a quick one with the Pauillacs, if you want to know," he said, because he could feel that his wife was waiting for an answer too.

"You could have let us know, rung us," she said.

"Jean," he said, "could you take a bottle over to the Pauillacs to thank them. I haven't got time today."

Jean knew this meant that he was embarrassed and he was sending him, Jean, to make this gesture because he didn't dare show his face. He allowed himself a few moments of distant compassion for this man who was getting old now and who had made this request with a gruff awkwardness which was ultimately touching.

The telephone. He wouldn't have been able to say why but it was the first thing John thought of when he woke. He had had a go at Georgia because she never rang him at Mark's flat when he was in London. If only he had a mobile, she could have rung him in the barn; it would have been almost funny and he could have invented all sorts of things about his meetings in London without taking his eyes off the house. He was going to have to ring while Georgia was out and leave a message on the answering machine to say he wasn't contactable. The nearest telephone box was right in the middle of Villars. Unthinkable. As for the next one, it was, at best, twenty kilometres away.

But, in order to alleviate his anxiety momentarily, he was granted a miracle. He heard the kitchen door opening and saw Georgia coming out, dressed, refreshed and ready for the day. He watched her as she walked out of the yard and waved to someone who was not in the field of vision afforded by the skylight of the barn. He recognised old Mother Pauillac's voice.

"You got back all right, then. It's not as if it's far."

"No problems at all."

"You know, you mustn't mind Desjean, he's not very often like that. He's a good sort really, you know."

Even Madame Pauillac didn't really believe what she was saying but she had to find something to say.

"No, no, it was fine."

"Are you going somewhere?"

"To Ribérac."

"Oh, well you'll be gone a while then. Have a nice time."

"Thank you."

And another little wave.

Ribérac. They never went to Ribérac. What had got into her all of a sudden? She can't have gone in for sightseeing now, surely. So last night she had been coming home from the Pauillacs'. Why not? But what was this story about Desjean who was a "good sort" at the end of the day, who had done something that "was fine"? He tried to put a face to this name, amidst all the confusion of the foreign sounds. He had to make a considerable effort in order for these new words to indicate a particular person. He repeated the two syllables which meant nothing to him until eventually he found it: the father and son, sullen the pair of them, that they sometimes saw in the village. Of course! They had bought the wood from them and the son had come to deliver it. He remembered clearly now. A *paysan*, muscly, with dark colouring and black hair and somehow not quite the strong, silent type. In all this remembering John still didn't manage to face the fact that Jean Desjean was good-looking, but the idea lurked somewhere in the background, making him feel sick while he thought back over the words that Georgia and Madame Pauillac had exchanged. "It was fine", "you mustn't mind him". He wondered again which of the two Desjeans they meant. He saw Georgia go over towards the car and then heard her setting off. Ribérac. He had at least three and a half or four hours ahead of him. At last. Unless old Madame Pauillac hung about round there all day. He would have time to nip into the house and do everything he had been wanting to do since he "left for London", he thought with a smile that was so joyless it was almost spiked with hate.

Bent double, he scuttled along the path that ran between the scarcely-opened barn door, and the courtyard in front of his house, and he slipped into the kitchen. As usual she had left without locking the door. He threw himself at a bottle of mineral water and drank half of it in two or three huge gulps, then he went and opened the fridge, grabbed some cheese (Roquefort, which would leave its smell on his hands for the next twelve hours) and he started to devour it as if he were seeing it for the first time. He bit into the bread, then ate an apple in just four mouthfuls. He felt as if he were suffocating, he was breathing very quickly but kept forgetting to take a breath between mouthfuls of food and drink. His blood froze. He heard some sort of movement behind him as if someone were pushing the door. He stood there petrified, one hand still full of Roquefort, the other clamped round the mineral water. Then he heard a growl which soon evolved into a timid bark. The dog! She'd gone out without the dog! And he could sense the animal the far side of the door. He put the bottle down and ran his hand through his hair. He opened the door and the animal started bounding in every direction, barking and wagging its tail in one of those demonstrations of affection which, for the first time, John found irritating. He pushed the dog away automatically while he thought about what he had to do. First, his clothes. He ran up the stairs and burst into his room as if he had come to put out a fire. He caught sight of his reflection in the wardrobe mirror and was almost frightened. The filth, the exhaustion and the beard had carved his face up between them. He had dark rings under his eyes and black marks on his forehead, probably dust. He stepped slowly towards himself, distraught at the sight. He wondered whether he was going mad; he certainly looked as if he were, so much so that it was almost comic. And, just at the thought of it, a lopsided smile played on his lips. His teeth were grey. He could have smacked himself. When he turned away so as not to have to see himself any more, he saw his bed, Georgia's bed, the white sheets slightly crumpled by his wife as she turned over in her sleep, there, all alone. She had not pulled the duvet up when she got out of bed. He leant towards her pillow, thought he recognised her smell and burst into tears, falling to his knees and grasping the fabric in his hand. After a few moments spent crying as silently as possible, he felt something wet and rasping on his cheek: it was the dog who had come to console him by licking him and sniffing him. John put his hand on his head, stroked him mechanically and smiled at the animal who put both front paws on his shoulders and went on licking his shirt, his hands and his face. He pushed him away and went to the cupboard to choose some clothes that he hardly ever wore and which would have been fine for London. He folded them carefully with the intention of putting them in a plastic bag when he went back through the kitchen. He took a shirt, a blue and white cotton sweater which, according to Georgia, didn't suit him but which would surely do, some clean socks and some boxer shorts. He thought briefly that sooner or later he was going to have to pick up the wretched suitcase, which meant finding the exact spot where he had left it. He had nothing left to do in the bedroom; he went back downstairs and saw the telephone. He thought back to what had been troubling him that morning, and frenetically dialled Jonathan's number, which he knew by heart. The dog was still at his heels, sniffing and circling, knocking doors and furniture with his wagging tail. While John listened to the telephone ringing, over there in London, the dog stood up on its hind feet and, leaning against his master's back, licked his ears. John pushed him down, muttering and swearing, and eventually kicked him. The dog went to sit in a corner and gazed at him piteously with something between sadness and reproach. After the fourth ring, John heard Mark's voice. It was the answering machine and John said: "Hello? Mark? You're obviously not there. It's me, John. I wanted to say I'm sorry I haven't rung you sooner.

I… I can't come to London this time. I've got a… um… a problem. A serious problem. But please, if Georgia rings, just tell her that I've gone out with um… some clients and that I'll call her back. Tell her everything's fine and you've seen me and everything. Please…"

At that point the answering machine stopped automatically. He redialled the number and picked up where he had been interrupted: "Yes, well, it's me again. That's it in a nutshell. It must seem odd. But I'll explain. It's nothing serious. Well, not too serious, but there you are. You see. Thanks. Bye. I'll call you back. Bye. Whatever you do, don't ring here. I mean at home, in France. Bye."

He listened to the messages on his own answering machine to see whether Mark had already rung. There was only one message, Helen confirming that she was coming for supper with Dave. It had been left the previous afternoon; Mark wouldn't have called before that and manifestly had not done so after that, either. At least that was one miracle in this whole business. Then the telephone started to ring. He stood there frozen to the spot, looking at the telephone, terrified without really knowing why. He was dying to know who it was. But he knew he mustn't answer it, so he went through to the kitchen. He was tempted to have a shower and to shave, or at least to brush his teeth. But he mustn't even think about it. Even if Georgia wasn't especially meticulous, she was nonetheless observant and she would certainly have been capable of detecting the signs of a brief passage through the bathroom, somewhere between the bottles of shampoo and conditioner, and the creams and even her own make-up (which he now knew she wore). Definitely not! He went back into the kitchen and then immediately doubled back on himself. He had nearly forgotten. A book. He slipped one into the inside pocket of his raincoat. Then he chose some food from the area that the locals would have called a cellar, a dark damp storage space behind the kitchen. He took some tins that

Georgia wouldn't miss, and a bottle of wine. There were three on the shelf. With a little luck she would think they had drunk more than she had reckoned when Helen and Dave came over. Anyway, she wouldn't be able to think of any other explanation, how could she possibly imagine what was really happening in her home? He must have spent not even a quarter of an hour burgling his own house, but he was afraid to stay on any longer, even if it was quite illogical to think that she would be back for a long while yet. But he couldn't really see himself switching on the television and casually making himself comfortable in an armchair. Yet he would have liked to. The dog was still there, he had got up and was trotting around behind him, following his every step. He shut him in the little room where the telephone was. And, equipped with his two shopping bags, one in each hand, with his food and the bottle sticking out of the one, and his clothes in the other, he went back across the yard in his raincoat and his suit, and into the barn. Even from there he could hear the dog barking, calling to him, whining and whimpering. He climbed back up the ladder and returned to the straw that was now his own, and in which like an animal he had hollowed out a bed.

He heard a scratching sound and the door below rattling, then more high-pitched yapping, like a muffled sneeze. He couldn't have shut the door properly and the dog must have followed him. The animal knew that he was in this barn and now he was barking. The whole village was going to hear him. John put his head in his hands and blocked his ears, he thought he might start howling himself. The sound of a motor in the distance. All these cars, these tractors, these machines, all these people who never stopped coming and going. He went back down the ladder with an agility he didn't know he had, jumped down to get there all the more quickly and opened the door. The dog leapt into the barn and jumped up on his hind legs. He was full of it with his dangling tongue and his stupid expression. He kept barking to express that excessive affection (which is exasperating because it is so unjustified) which all dogs feel for their masters. And he, John, stood there trying to sound strict as he just kept saying: "Gulliver! Gulliver! Be quiet. Down!" (Gulliver? How the hell did they come up with such a ridiculous name?) The dog was bounding backwards and forwards, and from side to side, he wanted to play, he was wagging his tail, he hurtled off to the far end of the barn, knocking over a pail which made a deafening metallic clatter, then he barked, braced with his muzzle near the ground and his tail in the air. John thought he heard footsteps outside. An illusion perhaps. John felt the same fear he had experienced the other night crossing the field in the rain, the fear of being discovered here like this or in his own house, his own kitchen. He gritted his teeth and growled like a dog himself as he asked the dog once more to be quiet. His fear turned to a raging anger, something he had never felt towards the dog before. He took three steps, the animal escaped his grasp, still playing. That was when he grabbed the wooden-handled sledge-hammer. He raised it. It was only to threaten the dog, he would think later. Then, no longer really knowing what he was doing, he brought it crashing down on the animal's head. He heard a strangled yelp, the dog scrabbled with his paws and twisted convulsively. He struck him again, a dull thud, the cracking of the setter's long fine skull. Then he hit it twice more, frenziedly. When he stopped the dog's head had disappeared, all that was left of it was a seething red mass dotted here and there with white and blue-grey hairs. He let the sledgehammer fall to his feet, and looked at his dog's body. After a few moments, during which he may have tried to take on board what it was he had done, he went over to the corner of the barn to be sick. He didn't have the strength to climb back upstairs, and he sat down on the matted straw mixed with dust and horse dung, just a few metres away from the headless setter. And for the second time that day he started to cry as silently as he could.

"Jean!"

He turned round abruptly because there was something threatening about this cry; people never spoke like that when they were just greeting him. He turned and saw Louis in the doorway of the shed where the goats were kept. He stopped the grain mill after a moment's hesitation which could easily have passed for rudeness. The rubber belt gradually slowed and eventually came away from one of the wheels. He wiped his forehead, leaving a black mark on it, and then rubbed his hand on his trousers. He still hadn't spoken, just nodded his head as he wondered what Louis had come for.

"Hello, how are you?"

"I need to talk to you."

"Oh?"

He hadn't even said hello.

"About what? If it's to buy some of these, you'd do better to talk to my father."

"It's not to do with the animals, it's something else. And you're going to have to talk to me, I'm not leaving here without some sort of answer."

Jean Desjean raised his eyebrows and dug his hands into his pockets with a slight shrug.

"You or your father, you're up to something, I want to know what."

Jean didn't move, he didn't bat an eyelid but he met the other man's eye, and as he stared at him he wondered what he could possibly mean. Had he seen the old boy going into the English couple's house too? Or was it something else altogether that Louis himself didn't know anything about?

"What are you on about? Are you turning detective now?"

"You just watch it, Jean. Don't mess with me."

"Hey, hey, who d'you think you are, coming and talking to me like that? Are you threatening me?"

"Tell me what's going on!"

"*What*, what's going on?"

"Just tell me."

"Shit."

"You'd better watch it because, believe it or not, you've been seen giving your father a good hiding."

"And is that any of your business? For a start, he's not my father. He's a bloody waster. But, please, keep your nose out of my life. D'you understand?"

"And what the hell was he up to on the road to Saint-Jean?"

"What do I know about it?"

Louis could see that there was nothing to be gained. He didn't want to mention his sister. Because he was beginning to wonder whether the boy was involved in some way.

"You just watch out, though, I tell you."

"Watch out for who? For what?"

"Not so much for me, you poor bugger, but for your father."

"My father's dead."

"You know what I mean. It's a shame you won't talk to me, Jean," Louis concluded on a gentler note which left Jean feeling slightly perplexed.

How much time had elapsed? He wouldn't have been able to say, he hoped something would draw him out of his torpor, he was hazily aware that he ought to move, to do something, to go even further with this absurdity, this crime and this filth, but above all he had to escape from this immobility. There he was, still waiting, sitting on the floor with his legs stretched out in front of him, his arms hanging by his side like a village idiot, in his suit and his raincoat, looking like a forlorn jumping jack, an old puppet languishing at the back of an attic, gathering dust. Then what he wished for with all his heart happened. A sound, a creaking, a crunching, a grinding which made him look up and cast his eyes over the dog's carcass. This sound brought home to him the fact that life was still going on outside the barn, reminding him that he shouldn't have been there and that he would have to go on hiding especially as he had just killed – even if it was only an animal. If only Georgia had taken the dog with her... he had seen that she didn't look after the animal properly when he wasn't there. Poor Gulliver. Another sound outside. He got up. If Louis came into the barn... or someone else did. It didn't matter who. He grabbed one of the dog's hind legs and dragged the body along the ground, as if it were just a hunk of meat, as if he had already forgotten that this was his own dog he was manhandling. He continued under the effects of mounting rage as he thought of Georgia's negligence, as if it were her fault, as if she had forced him to kill the dog. Still holding his burden by one paw, he began to climb the ladder. Blood dripped on to the dust; he would have to come back later to muss the floor up and hide any traces of it. He climbed a rung at a time, and heaved the body up. He took it to the far end of the barn, by the wall, far enough from the place where he had chosen to hollow out his bed. He covered the dog with straw and went and sat down as far away as possible, because he was now frightened of this carcass with which he shared his refuge.

Jean Desjean thought over what Louis had said. He had been wrong to react as he had, but the man had set about him all wrong. Who on earth could have seen him laying into his step-father? Louis himself? Possibly, because he was always nosing around. But it wasn't his style to hide his light under a bushel; if he had seen them, he would have said so. He glanced over towards the trees on the other side of the hill, up above the meadow dotted with a neighbour's cows. There was no one to be seen. From time to time you could hear a crow cawing, cattle lowing, the droning of a distant engine, but everything seemed deserted, and yet you couldn't go anywhere in this place without being seen. Even he, who spent his life hiding, saying nothing and glowering at everyone... he sometimes suspected every inhabitant in the area of knowing his most intimate secrets. He didn't feel like talking to anyone, and when all was said and done, there wasn't any point anyway, if even people he would never have confided in knew everything. He lowered his head and gave a good kick to a clod of earth before taking a deep breath and letting out a sigh. Louis was warning him against his stepfather. Well, that was rich! He had such a big mouth. He always thought he knew everything. All the same... Jean himself didn't understand his almost defensive reaction to the old boy. He could have killed him, he knew that, he realised that, but he didn't want all these people you couldn't see but who hung about in the woods and the fields, the villages and towns, to get involved. He stopped thinking about it before he was forced to admit that he might just feel some affection for the old man, and that if he ever did kill him it would be with... compassion? Regret? Love? The right word would never come to him.

Rats, crows, bats, worms, a whole menagerie of real and imagined creatures came to mind now that he was living a few metres from a corpse, because Gulliver, his own dog, had now joined that world, had become part of that fauna. John sat huddled in his corner of the barn, looking out of the window to his house where there was still nothing going on. He didn't dare turn to look at the dog's tomb of straw; he was afraid he might see or hear all these creatures which lived off death, as if the dog, which had become this headless thing, was calling to them. He looked at his watch, it was five o'clock. Georgia still hadn't come home, but at least the hands on the watch face evoked a reassuring reality, timings, hours, minutes, the rhythm of normal days. He went down to the ground floor to get away from the infernal animals hovering over his dog, and to light a cigarette.

He wanted to open the bottle of wine he had brought back from the house, but he realised he hadn't remembered the corkscrew. It was far too late to go back along the path across the yard, and go back to the kitchen. Unlike the locals he didn't carry a knife in his pocket. He tore off the red plastic from the top of the bottle and sat staring at the cork like a monkey undergoing an intelligence test in some laboratory. He walked round the barn, looking for an alternative tool. He felt angry with himself, and then with farm workers for not leaving corkscrews in barns, with Georgia for no precise reason, unless it was just that she had his corkscrew and it was her imminent return that meant he couldn't get it. In the end, in his anger, he broke the neck of the bottle against the wall. The wine ran over his fingers and shards of glass fell to the bottom of the bottle. He didn't have any sort of drinking vessel either. He put the top of the bottle against his lips, making an effort to avoid cutting himself. The wine gushed over his cheeks, his chin and his neck, leaving long red streaks on his shirt. Then he thought that he would be coming home from London the next day and he was going to have to wash.

He emptied the bottle very quickly and went back up the ladder, soothed by his drunkenness. He talked to himself, but quietly so that no one would hear him. Then he went to sleep.

Louis went into his mother's house without knocking. First he saw her from behind, as she almost always was, with her shoulders hunched, busy with some mundane task that she performed without thinking about it. She didn't even turn round as she asked: "Where've you been?"

"Well, at home, would you believe. Is the old man in bed?"

"No, no. In Thiviers."

"At the café, then."

"You're a fine one to talk. D'you want some coffee? It's still nice and hot."

Dragging her slippers along the ground and drying her hands on a cloth knotted at her waist, she went over to get the coffee which had been reheated so many times.

"It's not strong enough."

"Is there anything else you want to complain about, while you're at it?"

"I'll make you some coffee myself, the right way."

"You do that."

"So, any news?"

"We had the Englishwoman to supper last night."

He slowly put down the Pyrex glass full of coffee, which he held with the spoon still in it, wedged between his first and second fingers.

"And what about her husband, wasn't he here?"

"He's in England, for his work."

"How long ago did he leave?"

His tone of voice had changed and she noticed straight away.

"Why d'you ask?"

"It just came out. How should I know?"

She knew her son well enough to know that he was lying to her, but on the other hand she couldn't bring herself to believe that he was sniffing around "Madame Georgia". She still hadn't given any reply, but he was reluctant to repeat the question.

"Desjean was there too."

"Where?"

"Here, last night. Drunk as a lord."

"What was he up to? Did you ask him to supper?"

"D'you really think we would? He invited himself."

She didn't want to encourage her son's dislike for their neighbour, but his parting words had left them ill at ease.

"He said there were people prowling around."

"You bet there are!"

"In the woods."

"Yes, that's right. Was the Englishwoman all right?"

"What makes you think she wouldn't be?"

He had a ready answer: "Because I think her husband's dead. Or he's killed your daughter." But he kept it to himself.

John was woken by a cry which seemed to be part of his dream. "Gulliver! Gulliver!" He found it difficult opening his eyes, and realised that he was still drunk. There it was again, "Gulliver! Gulliver!" John put his head in his hands. And despite the fact that he was drunk, which – along with the absurdity of this new life – made everything seem somehow distant, he grasped the fact that Georgia had come back from Ribérac without his hearing her, and that she was now looking for the dog. A note of anxiety distorted Georgia's voice, making it more shrill, more urgent. "Gulliver! Gulliver!" Then it became tinged with anger. She cursed the dog, more to reassure herself than anything else, to convince herself that he had just done one of those "silly" things that make life so difficult. It was dark. But there were still glimmers of grey lighting up the night with the help of the moon. John turned on to his stomach and wriggled over to the window. There she was, standing in the middle of the path. She kept looking from right to left, she had taken her coat off. She didn't know which way to head to look for the dog.

"So, have you lost your dog?"

A man's voice, a strong voice which resounded in the darkness, some stranger, almost shouting; then he recognised the voice of the Pauillacs' son.

"I must have not shut the door properly, and he must have opened it on his own. He must have wondered where I'd got to and gone looking for me."

She was clearly close to tears, because her feelings of guilt had started to mingle with her anxiety.

"Don't upset yourself, he'll be back."

"I've heard that people sometimes steal them. He's a proper gun dog, you know."

"Yes, I know. But at this time of night… No, he won't go far, don't worry."

And as he reassured her he started to think that a dog disappearing and a brand new suitcase in the middle of the woods with the husband's clothes in it was a bit much.

"But a dog like that can go for miles."

"You're not going to look for him at night, though, are you? Come on."

"What am I going to do?"

"He'll come back, I'm sure he will."

And from his window John watched Louis put his hand on Georgia's shoulder as she started to cry.

"Come on, come on, sh!"

"Oh God, what if he doesn't come back?"

Louis could feel the general impatience that he felt for everything getting the better of him, and he started to talk more abruptly: "Listen, I know everyone around here, if someone finds your dog, I'll know about it. If you like, we can go and look for him together if he's not back in the morning."

"Would you do that for me?" she asked as she wiped her eyes with the back of her wrist.

"Yes, come on. Go in now."

He felt there must be some connection between his discovery of the suitcase and the dog's disappearance, but he couldn't begin to work out what it might be. Georgia took his advice and went back into the house, with her head lowered, watched by John, who had recently killed their setter, and not thinking for a moment that she should ask Louis in for a drink. The latter was wondering whether she might not have killed her husband, the Englishman. He suspected women of being capable of that sort of thing: killing their husbands and weeping over their dogs.

From John's point of view, he had heard that they would set off to look for Gulliver the following morning. He wondered whether this *paysan* was up to something himself, even though he realised that he could hardly have any recriminations for any-one but himself that particular evening. But it was stronger than him, and he was forced to conclude that his own crimes could in no circumstances justify those that others might intend to commit. He went back to sleep, burying himself as far as possible into the straw.

Georgia was sitting in the kitchen. She had poured herself a glass of neat whisky, which was unusual. Now that the dog had disap-peared, she looked at the walls and the things around her differ-ently. The sewing machine stood at the far end of the table, silent, almost reproachful. A mountain of fabric was piled on the chair next to her, rich, thick, heavy fabric from which she was to make curtains. She didn't have the strength to set to work now, she listened out for every sound in the night as if the dog might come back at any moment. She felt as if something else were missing, something other than Gulliver. A little detail which was only irritating because it wasn't there. She thought back over all the events of the day, her trip to Ribérac, and it felt as if her life in the Dordogne was just a tiresome weight around her neck, an absurdity. Perhaps it was this last word which reminded her what it was that was missing, and she couldn't help a sad little smile spreading over her face: she was waiting to hear the little noise made by the mouse, nibbling the walnuts in the cellar.

Just one more day like this. That was John's first thought when he woke up. Tomorrow he would be going home and he had a lot to do to prepare for his return. Most importantly, he needed to wash and shave. Tomorrow evening he would have a bed, a fire in the hearth, a glass of whisky in his hand, he would smoke a whole packet of cigarettes in one evening, he would eat like a horse. He was excited at the thought of it and, despite being exhausted, it gave him a new surge of energy. He was almost tempted to laugh. Then the thought of the dead dog came back to him. He had killed Gulliver. His feelings of remorse dampened his mood. So he made some resolutions and made himself some promises. He had come close to madness but he wouldn't go there again. He would go back to London in a fortnight's time, and work himself to the bone, so much so that his work would be like a punishment, to find forgiveness in his own eyes. Poor Gulliver. And he would be especially attentive to Georgia. He had misjudged her. And, anyway, it felt so good, being all nice and warm with her in his own home. He loved her. He was almost overcome with impatience at the thought that in twenty-four hours, or a little more, he would be back in the normal world. He was tempted to pray and to thank the heavens like a hermit in the desert who finds grace at last.

Louis arrived in front of the house in his van and tooted enthusiastically because he was quite incapable of doing anything quietly. She was probably still asleep. Of all the English people who had come to live in the Périgord, he still hadn't met one who could get up before nine o'clock in the morning. I ask you.

But there she was. With bags under her eyes, but there all the same. She had slept badly, poor thing, you could see that. He opened the door and gestured for her to get in. The smell of wet dog stuck in her throat, but she sat down on an old brown paper flour sack which was meant to be keeping the seat clean. Syringes for the livestock cluttered the dashboard, along with an old Opinel knife and a red plastic gun cartridge which she picked up, intrigued by this instrument of death. "It's for roe deer," explained Louis. She put the cartridge back down with a hint of disgust, then she looked round behind her and saw a brown leatherette case which could only have been for a gun.

"Is that a gun?" she asked.

"It's my rifle. Semi-automatic. Four shots. I've had it since I was fifteen. It's a nice one." And he kissed the tips of his fingers to demonstrate just how nice his semi-automatic was.

"Right, let's go," he said and he put the van in gear noisily, leant forward over the steering wheel as if he were pushing the thing with his own shoulders, and they set off.

He had had an ingenious idea. He would tell Georgia that he had decided to come home a day early. He couldn't hold out any longer. He would tell her that his work had gone particularly well in London and that, in his impatience to see her again, he had cancelled his meetings for the last day. And caught the night train. He grabbed the plastic bag with the clothes that he had stolen from himself the day before.

It was risky but he didn't have any choice. Louis's van had only just gone out of sight when he half opened the barn door, glanced out at the path and sprinted over to the house. Out of some monstrous reflex he took great care so as not to let the dog out before remembering that his body was rotting in the same place that he himself had slept. He went into the bathroom and ran some hot water in the basin. A delicious sensation as he felt his fingers warming up. He washed his face and brushed his teeth, the minty flavour of the toothpaste seemed really exquisite. He shaved very quickly, cutting himself all over the place. Then he burned his skin putting on an excess of aftershave. He rediscovered artificial fragrances. He had to have a shower. He looked at his watch. It was quarter to nine. He had forgotten to check the time when the Pauillacs' son and Georgia had left to look for Gulliver. He undressed and put his suit and shirt in a pile on the floor. He had left the raincoat in the barn. He had a shower, soaping himself energetically. He could have stayed under the shower for hours. But his own fear forced him to get out quickly. Just changing his smell and wetting his skin was enough for him to pass from one world to the other, and he couldn't get over it. As he stepped out of the shower he looked at himself in the mirror. He had lost weight. Of course he had. He had hardly eaten anything for three days. He put on his clean clothes and went to look for some shoe polish in the utility room. He could quite easily wait for her there. If she checked the timetables she would probably discover that there wasn't a train that could possibly have got him there then, but it was highly unlikely that she would. He picked up his suit with a grimace of disgust, as if it were an old skin sloughed off by a snake. There were a few embers in the fireplace; he burned his jacket and trousers, his shirt, his socks and his underpants. The whole room stank of burnt fabric. He opened the door and let in the cold air.

Georgia was trying to find something to hold on to while Louis sped along the tracks through the woods. From time to time he looked to one side and mentioned whatever memories a particular place held for him, a stag he had killed, a girlfriend he had met up with, then he would give Georgia a little smile and a wink. And at regular intervals he would say: "He can't have gone far." At the same time he thought of asking for news of John but didn't know how to go about it so that his curiosity wouldn't be misinterpreted. He could tell that, despite his chattering, she was still worrying about her bloody dog. And she would say: "We'll have to go a bit further, that sort of dog can go a long way without tiring. He's a gun dog." And off they would go again. She explained to him, for at least the third time, that setters were gun dogs. He should know. He was president of the local bloody shooting club.

She couldn't believe that he could drive along these muddy tracks in his van like some delivery man in London.

"We're nearly in Saint-Jean here," he said. "My sister lives a bit further on, over there, in the middle of the woods. Something and nothing, that is. Not worth as much as the skin off a rabbit's back."

"What? Her house?"

"No, her."

He talked of her in the present tense. People weren't supposed to know that she was dead, and, at the same time, he was testing Georgia's reaction. He talked all the more harshly about her because he now resented the deceased for going and playing this trick on him before they had had time for a reconciliation, abandoning him to his own feelings of guilt and a sense of failure.

"Is the house in the middle of the woods? It must be pretty."

"You can say that again."

"Can we see it?"

That was all he needed.

"If you like, but we're not stopping, because my sister and me... we don't really get on."

"Really?"

She would clearly have liked to know more but she, quite rightly, thought she ought to leave it there. Then she was thrown forward and almost hurt herself on the dashboard as he slammed on the brakes. (He had already explained that safety belts were useless.)

"Did you see him? Did you see Gulliver? What's going on?"

He didn't answer. He reversed at break-neck speed. He was looking dead ahead with an expression somewhere between fury and perplexity, the sort of look he might have worn when he was out hunting and he thought his prey was about to get away. He had come within sight of his sister's house and had recognised old Desjean's car parked outside. Georgia hadn't noticed anything, but the door had opened and Desjean had stepped out. He had looked to left and right like a man with a guilty conscience. Louis knew too much about the woods and about people for there to be any doubt about what he had seen, and a man like himself, who knew about hunting down his prey, needed only a few seconds to understand what this creature he didn't like had been doing there.

He leant forwards with both elbows on the steering wheel, his sleeveless leather jacket making him look as if he had enormous shoulders, and he scowled and twisted his lips as if he were moving an imaginary piece of straw from one side of his mouth to the other. Desjean had been wearing his blue jacket unbuttoned over his white vest. He had gone back into the house quickly enough.

"What are we doing?"

"What?"

"What are we doing?"

"We're going back, we're not going to find your dog today."

"Really? What about your sister's house?"

"We went past it just now, didn't you see it?"

"No."

"Well, it was there, all right. It's not that interesting."

Georgia couldn't understand why he was closing up suddenly and she wondered whether she had said something wrong.

Louis, meanwhile, was thinking about Desjean, and about Héloïse and about the body that had been left by his door. A bullet unleashed on its own, a mistake... now that would be some hunt.

She crossed the yard with her head down and, still looking at her shoes, she shut the door and sensed a presence. She stifled a cry when she saw the silhouette slumped in the armchair, snoring slightly; then she recognised John. She moved towards him carefully as if she had just come face to face with a vision and she was afraid it might evaporate. Then she touched his arm and whispered "John". He opened his eyes and looked up at her in blind panic. For perhaps two seconds he thought he was still in the barn and she had caught him. Then, just as quickly as she had recognised him, he remembered his present situation and the speeches he had prepared, and he even took the time to rub his eyes.

"John?" she said, frowning, as if she were asking if it really was him here in front of her.

He smiled broadly at her, pulled her over to him on the armchair, sat her on his knee and kissed her gently.

"But I thought you were coming home tomorrow?" she asked after the first demonstrations of affection.

And he smiled again.

"I travelled overnight," he said. "I'm pretty knackered, but it was worth it."

He hoped that at this stage she would at least offer to make him some coffee. Instead, she burst into tears and just managed to say: "John, Gulliver's gone."

"What do you mean?"

"I've lost Gulliver. He's gone. I went to get something in Ribérac." (He noted that she hadn't even lied about her unusual destination). "To Ashley's house." (The curtains! Now he understood.) "And when I got back he wasn't here. I've looked everywhere. I can't find him."

Her face was streaming with tears and her cheeks were bright red.

"But how did it happen?" he asked, giving a more than acceptable impression of concern mixed with bafflement.

"I don't know. I can't have shut the door properly."

"I can't believe it."

"Oh, it's my fault, I... I..."

He put his hand on her head and drew her against his shoulder as he heaved a slightly impatient sigh, their combined effect implying that he was prepared – at considerable personal cost – to forgive her extraordinary and culpable incompetence. At the same time he was extremely busy trying to forget that he himself had shattered the animal's skull with a sledgehammer. After a surprisingly short period of time, he almost managed it. But she was in such a state that he was the one who had to go and make the coffee. He couldn't believe that after the hell that he had been through, he was the one who had to cheer her up and tend to her. She did eventually calm down after three or four cigarettes and as many cups of coffee. He almost couldn't wait to churn out all his lies to get it all over and done with, and start a normal life again. The time had come.

"You'll never guess what happened to me at Waterloo last night."

"What?" she asked in a relatively neutral tone.

"I had my suitcase stolen."

"Really?" (Still the same tone of voice.)

"Can you believe it?"

"But how did they do that?"

"I fell asleep in a waiting-room — I said I was knackered — and when I woke up, my suitcase had gone. All I had were the clothes on my back."

"Was there a lot of stuff in your suitcase?"

"My work clothes. My suit, that sort of thing."

"But you usually travel in your suit."

"Yes, but this time I was travelling at night, I wanted something more comfortable. But, you see, that's what England's like nowadays, the crime rates, danger round every corner, when you think…" and he launched into some recent British crime statistics which she already knew because she had heard them on Radio 4.

"What are we going to do?"

"About what?"

"About Gulliver?"

That bloody dog again, but he couldn't exactly shout out that he was dead, that it was a shame but that… but that… they could get another one or something. So he gave up another half hour to reassuring and consoling her while she explained that Louis, the Pauillacs' son, had kindly helped her look for him. He didn't dare ask her whether Louis had made advances to her or tried to maul her, but that didn't stop him thinking about it.

"Have you seen Desjean?"

"No, not for a while. What do you want him for?"

Standing behind his bar, Maurice could tell from Louis's tone of voice that he didn't just want to see him for some buying or selling of livestock. And since his last visit to the Desjeans when he had found the youngster all on the defensive, he had hesitated to show his face there. And now there was another reason too.

It was raining outside, the gas heater gave off a thick, slightly suffocating smell. Two *paysans* were sitting up at the bar, leaning over their glasses and watching Louis over their shoulders without actually daring to turn round, as if they were afraid to talk to him.

"Are you having a drink?"

"No."

That wasn't normal either. Louis turned back to the window where the hazy condensation blended with the grey of the sky and the bland façades of the houses opposite. He didn't want to see them either, the barman and the other two. Still that same feeling that everyone knew everything. Without having to breathe a word. That was probably why they kept saying "you still don't know the half of it" or "you haven't seen the worst of it" when they were talking, as if to convince themselves that it was true. But these three could easily know that Héloïse was dead, who had killed her and that he, Louis, had buried her. And that heavy silence, painfully, awkwardly broken by the odd sound of a glass moving or a mouth slurping, that silence said all that. And, despite the fact that Louis was born in the village, he couldn't bear to meet their eyes at that precise moment.

He yanked the door open, without saying goodbye and with one hand still in his pocket. As he came out of the café he saw the Englishwoman's Peugeot estate. It was her husband back from London, if he had gone there at all. If he hadn't killed Héloïse. He even wondered whether the English couple had joined forces with Desjean to kill his sister. It was possible, even if it didn't make any sense.

"Do you think we'll find Gulliver?"

They were sitting in an expensive restaurant in Champagnac-de-Belair, celebrating John's premature return.

"I feel so guilty being here," she said, drinking some of the excellent white wine and lighting a cigarette, "while the poor dog's all alone in the woods. He must be really frightened."

"He *is* a gun dog, you know. Instincts, you know, um… I don't know how to put it. But he'll find his way home soon enough. Definitely. He might even be there now."

He went on in this vein, inspired by the warmth of their surroundings and by the abundance of food and drink, and Georgia was beginning to let herself be convinced by his assorted arguments. She had chosen *foie gras* as her first course. Then he told her about his short stay in London, about problems in the property market, the unbearable atmosphere that hung over the English capital… and he asked her how she had spent her week.

"Did you see anyone?"

"Helen and Dave came one evening."

"Did they?"

"And I went over to Ashley, like I said."

The main course arrived.

The comfort afforded by his well-padded chair would have been enough to intoxicate him but he helped himself along the way by drinking twice as much as her.

"When are you going back to London?"

"I don't know yet. I've had enough of London."

"Do you want to give it up?"

"No, no. I… um…"

"And what about money?"

He made do with a neutral shrug. The lamb was perfectly complemented by the Pécharmant, and he thought Georgia looked ravishing. He almost regretted that he couldn't tell her the truth about the last few days. The only true adventure of his life. It was almost comic. They could have laughed about it together. Then he remembered that he had killed the dog. He had a bit of trouble with his dessert, but that may also have been because he was no longer used to eating so much.

He pretended to work all through the following week, revelling in a combination of laziness and an indefinable feeling of anxiety. He would take the car and say he was going to see properties that warranted a closer inspection. He would stop in cafés and drink a couple of beers, always under the suspicious eyes of the *patron* and a few other customers. This was his way of escaping from Georgia's darker moments when she suddenly went into mourning for Gulliver and blamed herself for his disappearance. There were the inevitable suppers, and an awkward moment when someone asked him what was on at the theatre in London at the time.

"I don't know, I didn't have time to pay much attention to that sort of thing."

"But what about the evenings?"

"I usually have supper with clients."

"But when you go past a theatre, don't you look to see what's on?"

Why were they making such a thing of it? What the hell did it matter to them what was on at the theatre, anyway, they were all stuck here in the country, penniless, and they wouldn't see London for months, years even, so...

"I'm not really into theatre."

He was treated to a raising of the eyebrows, but at least they left him alone.

One day in the middle of the second week he was woken by the telephone ringing; it was nine o'clock. He jumped straight out of bed because, for once, he hadn't had anything to drink the night before. He felt incredibly refreshed and full of energy, and although he didn't know what he would do with all this energy, he felt very glad of it. Georgia was already up and had picked up the telephone downstairs. He went down in his bare feet, and even the coolness of the wooden stairs gave him a sense of well-being, as if he had always led a healthy life. Then he heard Georgia saying: "No, I can't manage that. But I could next week. When John's in London. Yes, I'll have time then. Yes, I'll call you. Yes, goodbye."

She was looking at her feet, with a smile on her lips and a thoughtful expression, a sort of delight as she contemplated some pleasure in store. Then she saw him halfway down the stairs, and she jumped.

"Oh, you're up."

"Yes."

"Good morning," she said, putting her head on one side.

He didn't answer. He was ashen. And, making a huge effort to sound as neutral as possible, he asked: "Who was that?"

She hesitated for a moment, ran her hand through her hair. He felt as if she were laying on the charm a bit to stall or to make him think about something else. Eventually she replied rather haltingly: "It was Ashley, asking when I'll be able to make his curtains."

"Oh."

"Are you all right?"

"Yes, fine."

She had lied. He couldn't see why the fact that he was there should stop her from making curtains. One thing was sure, she was waiting for him to leave. He went through the motions of having breakfast mechanically, listening to the sound of the shower in the bathroom and forcing himself not to think of her naked body streaming with water. Then he thought that since his return she hadn't demonstrated a great deal of affection, quite the contrary. She had been distant even, when they were in bed together. As if she were saving herself for… for someone else, for example. The "cousin" of the first telephone call. When all was said and done, the worst sort of news always came by telephone, a contraption that only lets us hear half the truth. On the one hand, what she had said corresponded pretty well with the explanation she had given him. Why didn't he confront her to get it over with and to be quite sure. He could ask her: "Do you still love me?" She would say: "Of course I do", rather impatiently. And what if he asked: "Have you got a lover?", she would lie, then she would humiliate him and hold his jealousy against him. They lied to him at work, and Georgia lied to him at home. He decided that it had been ridiculous to think that he could uncover her unfaithfulness by watching the house for just three days. And, anyway, if she had a lover, she would see him the following week. She had said so herself on the telephone just a few minutes earlier. Georgia had come out of the shower, she was wearing nothing but a towel round her hips. He closed his eyes so that he didn't have to imagine another man touching her body, and carried on eating his cereal, which he found too filling. He scratched his thigh, got up and dragged his feet over to the sink to fetch a glass of water. The sky was grey and dark: morning could easily be confused for evening, the clouds looked like plastic bags swollen with rain which were ready to burst at any minute, and it would be months before this great quantity of water had finished falling on them. And there he was, cornered in this house with no views, living with this woman who was unfaithful to him, bringing back just enough money to survive by doing a job that didn't interest him. Her lover must be English because she had spoken in English. But that didn't mean anything. The "cousin", on the other hand, was French from what he'd been told. He couldn't remember. Perhaps she had several lovers. The image of her half-naked body flitted across his mind again. He put his head in his hands and rested his elbows on the table.

"What are you thinking about?"

He was thinking that the following week he would go back to the barn and watch her comings and goings so that he could catch her with her lover. But he couldn't exactly tell her that.

The few days that lay between him and his departure were devoted to minutely detailed, secret preparations for his expedition. He spent his time making mental lists of things he needed for his life in the barn: warm socks, a thick sweater, he didn't even envisage taking a change of clothes for his false return, so convinced was he that he would catch her out and have proof of her guilt. The terrible moment scrolled before his eyes, following a diversity of scenarios but always inflicting the same pain on him. He added to his luggage a knife and a flask full of whisky. He stored everything in a drawer reserved for summer clothes which were of no use to him at the moment and which he had stowed in the attic while Georgia was out. When everything was ready, he put his things into a bin bag and took them up to the barn in readiness one evening, the day before the dustbin men came, in fact, and even the clinking of bottles inside the black plastic sack didn't arouse any suspicion. He was most insistent that he could take the rubbish out on his own, telling Georgia that it was too cold and she should stay by the fire. She didn't take much persuading and he even felt slightly bitter about that. She really did treat him like a servant.

He climbed up the ladder and lobbed the bag up as if he were throwing a grenade out of a trench. A pestilential smell knocked the breath out of him, and he wondered what it could be, before realising that it must be Gulliver's rotting body.

On the day of his departure, John did all the things he usually did on those occasions, but excessively slowly. Even though the day before he had absolutely insisted that he wanted to catch the train at two minutes past eight. He couldn't find the trousers he needed – and which he himself had hidden under the bed, and he had a go at Georgia about them. There weren't enough clean socks. He made a mark on his shirt as he drank his tea, and decided to go and change "quickly". In the end, as he had hoped they would, they arrived at the station in Thiviers ten minutes after the Limoges train had left. He heaved a devastating sigh and decided he would wait for the ten o'clock train by himself in the café.

"I'll wait with you."

"No, it's not worth it," he replied, all generosity.

"I haven't got anything to do."

"No, really, it would just be a waste of time."

He was hoping to save on the taxi fare, at least between Bussière-Gallant and Thiviers. And he wanted to get back to the barn as soon as possible. His impatience seemed to imply, although rather vaguely, that he felt nostalgic about it, that he had never felt as free as he had lying there in the straw and the filth. He could see everyone, and no one could see him, no one even knew he was there. In the last week, when he had decided that he would definitely return to his observation post, he had sent a letter of resignation to London, asking them not to contact him. He hadn't asked for any remuneration, he just didn't want to be contacted. He thanked them for everything... etc. On a different but related subject, he had been in touch with a French loan company to deal with the problem of the overdraft.

"Don't you want me just to stay and have a cup of coffee?"

"Yes, OK, if you like, but I can't have you waiting for two hours."

He answered so aggressively that she lowered her eyes and asked hesitantly: "Tell me, John, have you met someone in London?"

He stood staring at her, open-mouthed, his arms hanging limply by his sides, with his new suitcase at his feet and wearing the new raincoat she had chosen for him.

"What do you mean?"

He knew exactly what she meant.

"Have you met a woman in London, John? Is there something going on… a fling, an affair? Oh God, the words!"

He suddenly felt as if he had blocks of ice instead of lungs. His heart had started beating faster, he wouldn't have dared look her in the eye – and at that very moment she was looking up, raising her eyebrows – because he could see that he was reacting guiltily, and he knew it himself.

"What makes you ask?"

"I don't know, you're so… distant, cold, irritable… I don't know."

This wasn't right, this wasn't right at all: she couldn't turn the tables like that. Everything he had done had been for nothing, now that she asked him this, now that she herself was having doubts. He stood there, watching her face and not saying a word. His hands were cold, so was his neck.

"If you've met someone, I'd rather you told me."

"Don't be ridiculous. I'm just worried about my work, that's all."

"You said everything was going well with your work."

"Come on, let's go and have a coffee."

They were the only customers in the huge room. They went and sat over by the window. Turning to look round, John thought he had never seen such a pitiful sight as Thiviers station in winter. It had started to drizzle and droplets ran slowly down the window, distorting the contours of everything that lay beyond. She toyed nervously with her cup of coffee and spilt some into her saucer. He took her hand. She thought for a moment that he was going to confess something to her.

"So?" she said.

"I love you, Georgia," he said.

She smiled at him a little sadly, almost as if she were disappointed.

Desjean stopped at the door to the Pauillacs' farmhouse as if he had come to a minefield. The air there always seemed somehow darker, thicker. He always slowed down when he crossed this yard, as the memory of Héloïse snagged on his heels, dragging him backwards, weighing on his shoulders. He looked over towards the barn, to what had been the pig sties, as if he expected something – he himself didn't know quite what – to come out of them. Then he heard a metallic sound. He thought it must be Louis repairing a tractor engine or sharpening a pick-axe. He could do everything, that Louis. He realised that the fear and loathing he felt for the man were tempered with admiration. And this thought led him to the conclusion that the same could be said for everyone else. Everyone who spat at Louis behind his back actually feared but admired him as well. In fact it was often the same people who came to look for him to sort out problems on their farms when they couldn't deal with them themselves.

His shoes made a deafening noise. He carried on towards the door. He was constantly terrified that he would end up admitting his crime, as if something inside him would force the words out of his mouth and he wouldn't be able to do anything to stop them reverberating around the four walls in front of all those people, or perhaps just one person. Héloïse's mother. That would be enough.

She was there, sitting at the end of the formica-covered table, doing nothing. That was already an indication that things weren't going well. She was sitting back on her chair with one arm on the table. He saw her in profile and could see her nylon apron clinging to the contours of her swollen stomach. He greeted her, almost shouting the local "*ko vaï*"; it was so loud in fact that it seemed ridiculous, as if he were trying to imitate Louis. Then, before asking anything else, he paused. He could have sworn she had been crying.

"Hey, is everything all right?"

"Do you want to see Louis? He's in the barn. He's mending a grindstone or something like that. To sharpen his tools, you know. He's keeping himself busy, poor thing."

He still didn't notice anything especially aggressive about the way she spoke to him, and he had been expecting this change in attitude for such a long time that he thought he would go mad and start howling.

"I came by to say hello. So there you are!"

"You'll have a *pineau*."

"Oh, all right then. And the boss, is he well?"

"He's well. He's keeping busy. But it's not the same any more. We're getting on, you know."

"Tch. And the neighbours?"

"Which ones?"

"The Englishman."

She settled for a shrug.

"He knows what he's up to, that one," went on Desjean, "with a part-time marriage. I shouldn't think he wastes his time over there. He has a taste for married women."

Another shrug. It was becoming increasingly clear that he would only be able to get her to talk about the English couple as the subject of jokes. And even then, it wasn't easy. But he was lucky because the "boss" had just come into the kitchen.

"Well, then, tch."

"So, are you getting a head start on drinking?"

"I came to see if you had any news. Where were you? You weren't over with your neighbour, were you?"

Old man Pauillac waggled his head.

"Are you going to join me?"

He didn't have much choice now. And he served himself a glass of *pineau*.

"How are the English couple then? I hope they weren't too annoyed about the other evening. Oh, my word, I really had a skinful!"

"Well, if you must drink so much…"

"Oh, and perhaps you never touch the stuff."

"She's taken her husband to the station, I've just seen them on the Villars road."

Now that he had the information he wanted, he realised he didn't actually give a damn. That particular game belonged to another era, a less serious time, in fact, when he hadn't yet killed the daughter of these two people who were now offering him a drink in their own home.

Georgia had waited until the ten o'clock train came. They had drunk coffee and smoked cigarettes. He hardly heard a word she said to him. There had been no more talk of betrayals and infidelities. They had exchanged banalities about their daily life, without drumming up a degree of enthusiasm which might, even artificially, have dispelled the uneasiness that had settled between them. He, anyway, didn't believe she was being sincere. She was only pretending to think he had a mistress in London. To make him feel more guilty. On the other hand, the things she had said on the telephone had been quite clear. She was waiting for him to go. For him to give her room to move. And since he had made his declaration of innocence, her attitude hadn't really changed, he couldn't say she had seemed to be moved by it. Perhaps she was even sorry that he didn't have a mistress because that would have freed her of any feelings of guilt towards him.

They parted company rather coldly as they would after a row that there hasn't been time to resolve. He had walked across the waiting-room of Thiviers station and headed for the platform.

If she had held him to her affectionately, if he had just glimpsed a tear in the corner of her eye, heard one gentle word, everything would have been different.

Desjean went and prowled round Héloïse's house once again then went back past Louis's house, as if by making this same trip a hundred times he would eventually erase his crime. It must be nearly midday. He headed back through the woods; the clouds had dispersed, and the sun threw a golden light through the dead leaves that still clung to the branches. That was when he saw him.

John had let the train leave; he had hidden in the station toilets. Georgia had not gone all the way to the platform with him. When he came back out, the people in the ticket office stared at him incredulously. He couldn't give a damn. He didn't know what to think any more, anyway. Even if Georgia saw him now, it didn't really matter. He went up the hill and went into a different café. He ordered a beer like the first time. But he didn't have the same wonderful feeling. He drank it quickly and asked for another one. He hadn't eaten anything and he already felt slightly drunk. He raised his arm and ordered a whisky. He was served without any kind of comment. They'd seen plenty of his sort in the cafés of Thiviers. He looked at the countless team flags and caps that lined the walls. A man with long hair, wearing chains and a biker's jacket, was drinking beer at the far end of the bar. John left after the second whisky. He was drunk. He found a taxi at the rank in front of the church and asked to be taken to Saint-Jean-de-Côle. He hung on to his suitcase the whole time as if he no longer knew it was there. In the taxi he used it to lean on. He walked through Saint-Jean without worrying that he might be seen, and followed the *route des crêtes*. He walked rather unsteadily but he still felt like drinking. He would happily have gone to one of the cafés on the square. He didn't really know what was stopping him. What it came down to was that he couldn't wait to get back to his barn and his straw, and perhaps even to being close to Georgia.

Desjean was below him when he saw him, and the old boy wondered what the arsehole was doing here when he was meant to be in London. And he had a good skinful. He saw him stepping sideways every now and then before recovering his balance. He couldn't hear very clearly but he thought the man might be talking to himself. In English of course. Old Desjean hid behind a tree. Then he started to follow him. He was used to it. That was exactly what you did when you went out hunting. It only remained to be seen exactly where he would lead him, this English prat. He eventually decided to go back to his car and wait in the village. That was the only place he could be going. He hurried down the hill, got back to his Renault 4 and took the lower road. He was bound to get to Tierchâteau before the Englishman. He hid the car behind a barn and went and hid in Marcellou's vineyard, behind the wooden shed on the approach to the village. Sure enough, he saw him appear forty minutes later. Desjean still didn't understand why he was making his way back on foot, if he had been taken to the station that same morning. He noticed that the Englishman had got rid of his suitcase.

John decided that the time had come to go along the road but still using the shelter of the trees, and he went a little beyond the edge of the woods as he made his way to the barn. He knew the way.

★

Louis had cleaned his gun the day before. It wasn't something he did very often. The gun had been needing it for some time. And as he carried out his work, he drank *pineau,* alone in the dark kitchen, using only the light from the next room. It was best like that. As if he were already hiding. Because that evening he had learned something for certain. He now knew who had killed his sister and who had tried to lay the blame at his door. In fact he had known for a long time. What had held him back from reaching this conclusion was that it struck him as so incredible. He drank another glass of *pineau,* downing it in one. Then he went and put the gun away in its old brown leatherette case. Four bullets. He yawned. Then he wondered what he was going to do with the pig which was still in his lorry. Another job that needed doing. It hadn't cost him much, but he needed to fatten it up now. He decided he should put it in the barn next to the English couple's house, them again, until it was ready to be slaughtered.

He had gone in through the back door. It still wasn't clear exactly what he was trying to do. But there was one explanation. The stupid bastard was spying on his wife. Old Desjean felt like bursting out laughing.

The stench was appalling. Particularly over towards the back wall, where he'd hidden the dog's body. Apart from this little detail, the barn felt familiar to him. And he had plenty of time, and he was well equipped. He started by unpacking the clothes he had prepared in advance and then changed. Like a professional putting on his work clothes. He took a deep breath and went over to the window for a first quick glance to remind him of the terrain, so to speak, before setting to work properly. Nothing moved. He lay down on his back and looked at the ceiling, counting the few holes that he could see by looking along the rays of sunlight that pierced between the tiles and lit up a few strands of straw or the dust on the walls.

"She was over at the Pauillacs."

"Who's that then?"

"The Englishwoman."

He had his back turned to Jean as he spoke; perhaps frightened that the boy might know that he was lying from his expression or from the way he moved. Jean was sitting at the table and old Desjean was looking out of the window. Out there, behind the building that was going to need reroofing one day, his wife was feeding the chickens.

"So what?"

"She told me she needed…"

He hesitated for a moment. He couldn't believe he hadn't prepared his lie a bit more. What on earth could she need?

"She needs compost. I told her we had some and that you'd take some over tomorrow."

Jean Desjean couldn't help delighting in the fact that he had an excuse to go over to the English couple's house. At the same time, the old boy must have had some sort of scheme in mind. Right now he was turning round and saying with a mocking smile: "Her husband's away on business."

Jean didn't say anything.

"I told her you'd drop by in the morning. She's going out shopping in the afternoon. I'll need the Renault 4, you can take the van."

"For a bag of compost?"

"Do as you're told, for God's sake!"

★

He immediately recognised Louis's van as it drew up right next to the barn door. Louis climbed out and slammed his door, making a sound like a tin can falling on the ground. He couldn't see him, but he could hear him talking to himself. Or perhaps he was talking to an animal, because John heard throaty growling sounds in response, which certainly couldn't have been a dog.

The barn door shuddered open, and John huddled down into the straw in the darkest corner. He could hear Louis saying, "Christ, what a stench!" then "Come on, you stupid bugger." A second growling sound followed by a piercing little squeal. John gathered that Louis had just brought a pig in. He started to sweat despite the cold. He envisaged Louis climbing the ladder for some reason which he couldn't for the life of him guess. Why did people in Louis's world climb ladders? He heard all sorts of noises he didn't recognise but whose origins he tried to guess at, and the words Louis muttered to himself helped to reconstitute the brutal gestures with which Louis unearthed various objects John had never been called upon to use.

After a few minutes and a loud "Right, there we are" which reverberated through the walls of the barn, the door shut and John was now in the company of a pig which trotted nervously up and down, grunting.

When evening came, Louis poured himself some pastis, alone in his kitchen. He tried to think over all of the things he had done secretly since he had discovered Héloïse's body, but soon this list was vying with another, the list of daily tasks that needed doing, as if he were trying to forget all the monstrous events that had coloured his life recently by intoning the infinite succession of chores like a prayer. The pastis gave him heartburn, providing something close to a distraction for a few moments. Then, without really thinking it through, he concluded that he kept making these lists so as to avoid carrying on the last, secret and criminal task that was still waiting to be done. He went to get his gun, took it out of its case, turned it over in his hands a couple of times and went up to bed.

8

Jean Desjean wondered whether nine o'clock wasn't a bit early for those sort of people. He shut the door of the van and the sound woke John. He went across the yard. Knocked on the door. She must be in because her car was parked outside the door. Jean wasn't used to the idea that one could go somewhere on foot. He knocked but there was no reply. He turned the door handle; the door wasn't locked and he saw this as a sign that he could go in without trespassing or any sense of impropriety, even if he had a vague feeling of guilt at his own line of reasoning, because he knew he was lying to himself. He looked at the mess their house was in, and smiled. She had even left a sharp knife on the kitchen table and beyond it the chicken carcass she must have picked at the night before.

He could hear the sound of running water from the next room. He went over towards it furtively. She was having a shower. He felt his pulse pounding in his temples.

John could feel the blood pounding in his temples too. From the window in the barn he had just seen this man walking into his house (at nine o'clock in the morning, far too early) as if it were conquered territory. He had been waiting for this moment, to have proof of Georgia's guilt before his very eyes, for days; but now he was praying to God that it wasn't true. He could have wept. He would have preferred not to be there, not to be seeing this, to have carried on loving Georgia without knowing anything.

He hardly heard the second vehicle which arrived and stopped in front of the barn. Louis's van. He went into the barn and shouted "All right!" to the pig, which had jumped to its feet when it saw him. Louis chucked a pan of grain on the ground for it, yelling "Eat that, you bugger". Then he went to fill the blue bucket with water. He stood with his hands in his pockets, leaning slightly backwards, watching the pig eating, and he thought that, as he had his gun with him to settle his score with the other bugger, he might as well do in the pig and bleed it on the same day.

That was when a third car made itself heard, slowing down as it approached the house. The driver climbed out while the engine was still running. He held the door open. It was old Desjean, and he started yelling at the top of his lungs, "So, are you still there fucking your little whore!" Then he got back into his car and drove off.

Georgia had stepped out of the shower with just a towel round her waist. She had jumped when she saw a man in her house, and she had been so surprised that she hadn't recognised him immediately. She had tried to hide her breasts with her hands and, as she did, she heard a call from outside which had plunged her into a state of panic.

Jean Desjean had heard it too. And it seemed to have rooted him to the spot. He couldn't understand what was going on any more. It was the old man's voice. He closed his eyes and thought he understood: the old boy had got him to come to this woman's house even though she hadn't asked him to, as a way of humiliating him, so that he could come and shout like that outside and make fun of him about it in future. But Jean was wrong. As he turned to leave, before he could even stammer his apologies to this half-naked woman, he found himself face to face with the Englishman, brandishing a sledgehammer.

★

Louis had seen him rushing down the ladder, falling to the ground, then getting back up like a wild boar leaping to its feet, picking up a tool without even looking at it, and going out of the barn, across the path and disappearing into the house.

There, in his own house, John had had time to see his wife half-naked in front of her lover. Everything that happened was like a continuation of the bad dream he had had the night before. First, the sledgehammer came down on Desjean's shoulder and he fell to the ground. The towel round Georgia's waist had slipped to the ground. She looked at this second apparition even more incredulously than she had the first and she cried "John? John?"; then the sledgehammer caught her full in the face.

Desjean had left straight after yelling his insults. Louis had cut across the path and the yard, following in John's footsteps, and, through the open door, he saw all three of them, bathed in blood. He stood open-mouthed in horror, holding his head in his hands and swearing quietly. The Englishman had a sharp knife planted in his back, his wife no longer had a face and Jean Desjean was unconscious on the floor, possibly dead too.

9

A sharp bang, with no echo. Someone was shooting. Then a second. Hunting big game. He suddenly realised that the season was over and that he hadn't seen anyone standing on point, waiting for the boar. Those were all Desjean's final thoughts. He realised that he was being shot, and he had no trouble guessing who was firing the gun, even though he couldn't see him. Then the windscreen shattered into a thousand pieces turning the woods, the sky and everything around him into a kaleidoscope of green and red.

"It could well have taken three shots," thought Louis before he took the last bullet back out of his gun. Then he got back into his van without even looking at the Renault 4, which had ploughed off the road and now lay on the verge like a dead animal. Now he was annoyed with himself for taking so long and hesitating so much. He should have done this sooner. Always late. Mind you, you couldn't be everywhere at once. Now, he had to go over to Saint-Saud to pick up a cow that was meant to be at the abattoir tomorrow morning. By five o'clock.

It was more than a week since he had had a call. But she had promised. He knew that he was in London that week. He wanted to see where she lived even though she preferred their meetings to take place at the chateau; she couldn't help being impressed by the setting and he had found it touching.

Ashley decided to do something rather unusual for him. He got into his car and headed for the village where she lived. He smiled to himself. He would never have guessed that he would become the lover of such a beautiful woman. It was probably even because he was ugly, because his body was so fat and grotesque, that he had been able to seduce her. To invite her to spend an entire afternoon in his house, in his bed. He knew that these things happened, but he didn't think he would experience them himself one day. And if her husband was there when he got there, he would say that he had been for lunch with Sue Brimmington-Smythe and had thought he would drop by to... umm, to let John know about a few properties for sale that might be of interest to his estate agency in London.

When he reached the village where John and Georgia lived he found the place sealed off by the police. Two dark blue vans were parked opposite a barn, and red and white tape had been put across the entrance to the yard. Ashley saw an elderly couple standing a little way away watching, then two more old women and another old man. He went over to ask what was going on. He noticed that one of the old women had tears in her eyes. The old man cleared his throat before telling him that it was the English couple's house and that apparently everyone inside was dead. It was his wife who had found them when she went to take them some eggs. He asked Ashley whether they were friends of his. He didn't answer. He stood in silence for a few minutes. Then, seeing the blue figures in their peaked caps, he decided to turn on his heels and leave as quickly as possible without any explanation.